A DECENT INTERVAL

A DECENT INTERVAL

A Charles Paris Novel

Simon Brett

CRÈME de la CRIME

This first world edition published 2013
in Great Britain and the USA by
Crème de la Crime, an imprint of
SEVERN HOUSE PUBLISHERS LTD of
19 Cedar Road, Sutton, Surrey, England, SM2 5DA.
Trade paperback edition first published
in Great Britain and the USA 2013 by
SEVERN HOUSE PUBLISHERS LTD

British Library Cataloguing in Publication Data

Brett, Simon.
  A decent interval. – (A Charles Paris mystery ; 18)
  1. Paris, Charles (Fictitious character)–Fiction.
  2. Actors–Fiction. 3. Shakespeare, William, 1564-1616.
  Hamlet–Fiction. 4. Theater–Fiction. 5. Detective and
  mystery stories.
  I. Title II. Series
  823.9'2-dc23

ISBN-13: 978-1-78029-044-7 (cased)
ISBN-13: 978-1-78029-539-8 (trade paper)

All Severn House titles are printed on acid-free paper.

Severn House Publishers support the Forest Stewardship Council [FSC], the
leading international forest certification organisation. All our titles that are printed
on Greenpeace-approved FSC-certified paper carry the FSC logo.

Typeset by Palimpsest Book Production Ltd.,
Falkirk, Stirlingshire, Scotland.
Printed and bound in Great Britain by
TJ International Ltd, Padstow, Cornwall.

To
Ali and Tim,
who know about the theatre

ONE

I t's been a while, thought Charles Paris. A while since I've been dressed as a Roundhead for a part. A while since I've had a part – any part, come to that.

Later in the day he would be dressed as a Cavalier. Because Charles Paris was fighting the Battle of Naseby. Alone. Still, it was work.

It had indeed been some time since he'd had any of that precious commodity, work, but then that wasn't unusual in what he laughingly called his 'career'. Like most actors, when unemployed, Charles Paris went into a kind of half-life. Yes, he met up with friends in the business, he continued to drink Bell's whisky either with them or more often alone, but the animating spark that made him fully alive was missing. And he kept wondering, as members of his profession in their late fifties tend to, whether he had already received his last ever job offer. An actor's career does not have a retirement cut-off point like more regulated types of employment. No farewell parties, gifts of carriage clocks and private pensions kicking in (few actors even know what the word 'pension' means). No, for them the end is a slow process of attenuation, six months of being offered no parts being followed by another six months of being offered no parts, and so on until the realization dawns that, yes, the moment of retirement did indeed occur, almost unnoticed, some years previously.

Charles Paris had therefore been extremely surprised to receive a call one Thursday morning in his studio flat in Hereford Road from the man who he supposed was still his agent, Maurice Skellern.

'Charles, how're things?'

'What things did you particularly have in mind?'

'Oh, work, you know, that kind of thing.'

'Maurice, if I had any work you of all people ought to know about it. You are my agent, after all.'

'Maybe, but you do hear of artistes who take jobs without telling their agents.'

'And have I ever done that?'

'Well, not in my recollection, no. But you do hear of these things. I mean, you know Edgar, the very clever boy I represent who's just finished a stint at the National and is now off filming with Tom Cruise—'

'No, I don't know him – and what's more I don't want to hear about him.' One of his agent's many annoying habits was going into excessive detail about the successes of his other clients while providing absolutely no work for Charles. 'Anyway, Maurice, to what do I owe the pleasure of a call from you out of the blue after eight months of total silence?'

'Eight months? Surely it hasn't been—?'

'Eight months,' Charles confirmed implacably.

'Well, everything's been very quiet in the business recently.' How many times had Charles heard that from his agent? 'Television budgets being cut back, the West End filling up with jukebox musicals or ones based on old movies. It's not a good time, you know. I mean if I hadn't got Edgar filming in the States and Adrian playing the name part in that cop series and Xanthe giving her Cleopatra at the RSC, I'd—'

'All right,' Charles interrupted. 'That's enough! I don't want to hear about your other clients. So once again I ask: to what do I owe the pleasure of this call?'

'Ah, well, something's come up.'

'Work?'

'Yes.'

'For me?' Maurice Skellern was quite capable of ringing Charles simply to crow about the fabulous contract one of his other clients had just netted.

'Of course for you, Charles.'

'What is it?'

'It's a television . . .'

Wonderful.

'. . . directed by Tibor Pincus.'

Even better. Tibor Pincus was one of the legendary television directors. Having escaped from Budapest when the Soviet tanks moved in 1956, he had quickly risen through the ranks of British television drama. He'd directed a play for ABC's *Armchair Theatre*, before joining the BBC and working on *The Wednesday Play*, a series which transmuted in 1970 into the *Play for Today* strand. Tibor Pincus had been at the top of his game at a time when the one-off play was one of the nation's glories, when it made headlines and prompted furious debate about the issues of the day.

Charles had had a tiny part in one of Tibor Pincus's productions in the early 1980s. He couldn't remember what the play was called, but it was one of the proudest entries on his CV – unlike his performance as Sir Benjamin Backbite at the Bristol Old Vic. ('In this Restoration comedy Charles Paris himself looked in need of restoration.' – *Western Daily Press*.)

Charles was touched that someone of the stature of Tibor Pincus should have remembered him (and surely there could be no other reason for this unexpected summons). He was also slightly surprised that the acclaimed director was still alive and working.

But most of all, he was extremely cheered and encouraged. The demise of the one-off television play had been much lamented over the years. Its time-slots had been taken over by endlessly recycling soaps and indistinguishable series set in hospitals, police stations or forensic pathology labs. Or, even worse, reality shows. Like most actors, Charles Paris had a deep-seated resentment for that form of entertainment. Pointing a camera at members of the public and waiting for them to make fools of themselves was not the highest form of art. But it was cheap, and television executives didn't care that such programmes put out of work a lot of actors and writers who might actually have produced well-crafted drama.

So the fact that a director of the stature of Tibor Pincus was back in business might herald the return of the single television play. That would be really good news.

'What is it?' asked Charles.

'What's what?' asked Maurice.

'The play, the part Tibor Pincus is offering me?'

'Ah, well there isn't actually a script.'

This was even better news for Charles. One of Tibor Pincus's great triumphs of the late 1960s, long before Mike

Leigh hijacked the form, had been a play called *Nexus*, built up by the actors through improvisation. It was still hailed as one of the landmarks of television drama.

If he was going to feature in a new improvised play by Tibor Pincus, then Charles Paris's acting career was about to take a very definite turn for the better.

Disillusionment had started to set in when Maurice Skellern told him that he was only required for one day's filming near Newlands Corner in Surrey. And that he was required to be there the next day, which was Friday. Dreams of Charles Paris being part of a long-planned masterwork by the great Tibor Pincus began to melt away.

It was a six a.m. call for costume and make-up. The car arrived in Hereford Road at four in the morning to pick up a somewhat frail Charles Paris. The excitement of having some work, combined with nervous uncertainty about what the work was, had led him to hit the Bell's whisky rather hard the night before.

He'd ended up slumped in front of the television, watching what was apparently some programme about the Wars of the Roses. It was the style of historical documentary which had become popular over recent years, in which modern-day footage was intercut by ancient documents and images, together with a minimal amount of costumed reconstruction, to produce a half-hour programme padded out to an hour which would have worked better on the radio.

The show was presented by a quite dishy woman with large breasts. Charles had read somewhere that she was a Professor of something at some university – and a feminist historian. She had written a book on changing attitudes to menstruation through the centuries, called *The Bleeding Obvious*, and appeared on *Newsnight* whenever a feminist guru was needed to pontificate on anything.

Knowing that she was a feminist made Charles feel guilty about being so aware of her breasts. For someone of his generation gender politics were a minefield. He had discovered the hard way that it was now all right to fancy women, but not to 'objectify' them. And being overly aware of the large

breasts of a television presenter he'd never met was danger-
ously close to objectification. He wasn't quite sure of the
politically correct approach for a man to a feminist with big
breasts. Probably to pretend not to notice them, that'd be safest.
Certainly not to look at them. God, it was sometimes difficult
being a man.

Anyway, he didn't like the documentary much. To Charles's
mind there was something ridiculous about the 1455 First
Battle of St Albans being discussed by a woman walking
through a shopping mall in modern St Albans. In what way
could the Tesco's, PC World and W.H. Smith she passed be
helping to give a historical context to her commentary? Also,
the cargo pants and tight cotton shirt she wore gave the mall
an impression more of a catwalk than a lecture room. Which
was probably the programme-maker's intention.

Charles did keep coming back to the fact that they were
very striking breasts, though. And he couldn't help feeling that
they must have had something to do with her success on the
box. He was sure that British universities boasted plenty of
equally knowledgeable academics whose less generous
contours kept them out of the nation's sitting rooms.

As he sipped at his glass of Bell's, Charles Paris, not for the
first time, pondered mournfully the impossibility of balanced
relationships with the opposite sex (though that, he reflected,
was probably too adversarial an expression to use – nowadays
no doubt you couldn't call women the 'opposite' sex, you had
to call them the 'complementary' sex).

He must have dozed off. The television was still on when
he woke, showing an early hours repeat of some talent show.
Called *StarHunt*, the series was apparently searching for an
unknown actress (or 'female actor', as Charles kept reminding
himself he had to say nowadays) to play the part of Ophelia
in a forthcoming West End production of *Hamlet*. The aspirants were amateurs – that was one of the show's selling points.
It was based on the – to Charles's mind completely fallacious
– view that anyone can become a star. All of the contestants –
girls in their late teens identically over-made-up with heavily
mascaraed false eyelashes and unnaturally white teeth – said
how big a part of their life *StarHunt* had become, how they

were 'really going to go for it', how much support they were getting from their families (cut to simpering parents in the studio audience), how nervous they were, and how much they respected their fellow contestants and the judges.

Charles was surprised to discover that this panel of D-list celebrities included someone he knew. Ned English, who would be directing the *Hamlet* when it finally got to the stage, was someone he had worked with. A very long time ago – about twenty-seven years – in Hornchurch, Charles had been in Ned's production of *Love's Labour's Lost* playing Costard ('Charles Paris's Mummerset accent was well-nigh incomprehensible' – *Romford Recorder.*) The director had then been an *enfant terrible* of the English theatre, notorious for stirring controversy by his 'reimaginings' of classic plays. While still at Cambridge, his *King Lear*, whose action had been transplanted into an aquarium, caused a minor sensation. And his *Doll's House*, in which all the characters were dressed like dolls and moved as if they were string puppets, was still talked about.

The *Love's Labour's Lost* in which Charles Paris had given his Costard had been set (for no very good reason) in the trenches during the First World War. When interviewed about his work, Ned English always said he 'listened to what the play was telling him'. If that was the case, Charles Paris reckoned that in *Love's Labour's Lost* the director must have been working from a different text of Shakespeare's play than the one he had.

As with most *enfants terribles*, Ned English's star had waned and he settled later in his career into comfortable predictability. A new generation of thrusting young directors hogged the limelight by doing things like setting J.B. Priestley's *An Inspector Calls* in a collapsing doll's house. (Damn, Ned had never thought of that.) Like Ned's, the approach of these new Young Turks demonstrated complete contempt for the text. This play, they seemed to be saying, is so bad that it can only be salvaged by my genius, my own particular brand of visual pyrotechnics.

So, having ceased to be flavour of the month, to get the job directing *Hamlet* must have been a considerable boost for Ned English. Particularly as it involved appearing on television.

Charles Paris was constantly surprised by the compulsive attraction of television to people in the theatre. Not the attraction of acting on the box – that was fine, and the money was much better than in the theatre. But so many actors and directors wanted to appear as 'themselves' (or rather a contrived version of themselves). They wanted to be on chat shows and panel games, showing how nice they were, how jolly they were. And very few of them were any good at it.

The idea of exposing himself in that way was total anathema to Charles. One of the reasons he had gone into the theatre was because the profession offered him opportunities to disguise his own personality under layers of others. He loved acting, but he shrank from revealing the real Charles Paris (or even a sanitized television-friendly version of his persona).

And yet Ned English was clearly glorying in his new-found fame on the box. In all such talent shows the mix of judges is the same. There's an acerbic pragmatist who is very rude to all the contestants. (In *StarHunt* this part was taken by Tony Copeland, a producer famous for his very lucrative touring productions and other wide media interests, who would be guiding the *Hamlet* on its trajectory into the West End.) There's a dishy young woman vaguely attached to show business who is sympathetic to 'how hard' the contestants have worked to get to this point in the show. And there's a lovable professional who is very encouraging, particularly when a contestant is patently rubbish.

It was this last role that Ned English had been granted. And he wasn't very good at it.

But he clearly thought he was. He played shamelessly to the camera, milked audience reactions and went through a laboured routine of defending the contestants from the cruellest (scripted) barbs of Tony Copeland.

This played perfectly into the producer's hands. So much so that Charles Paris began to wonder whether Ned had been given the job solely to point up the wit of Tony Copeland. The latter treated his fellow judge as an innocent child, who naively could see the good in everyone. A typical exchange between the two of them after an unfortunate aspirant had recited a Shakespeare speech would go:

PRESENTER: Well, Ned, what did you think of Kelly-Marie's performance of Portia's speech from *The Merchant of Venice?*

NED ENGLISH: I think the girl has a lot of talent. Clearly a bit of a problem pronouncing her Rs, but with elocution—

TONY COPELAND: I'd say a bigger risk for her was falling on her Rs.

[Audience laughter. Camera cuts to unfortunate aspirant, fighting back tears.]

NED ENGLISH: Now you're being cruel, Tony. As a director, I know that every actor can improve enormously with a little encouragement.

TONY COPELAND: I personally think it's cruel to encourage someone who has no talent.

NED ENGLISH: Are you saying Kelly-Marie has no talent?

TONY COPELAND: I've seen more talent in a plank of wood.

[Shocked audience laughter. Camera cuts to unfortunate aspirant, having even more difficulty in fighting back the tears.]

NED ENGLISH: Oh, that's just unfair, Tony.

TONY COPELAND: I agree. Yes, I apologize for what I said.

NED ENGLISH: I'm glad to hear it.

TONY COPELAND: Comparing Kelly-Marie to a plank of wood is definitely unfair . . . to planks of wood!

[Riotous audience laughter and applause. Camera cuts to unfortunate aspirant, now in floods of tears, being led away by a hostess in a sparkly dress.]

And so *StarHunt* went on, like all so-called 'reality shows', humiliating members of the public, an activity rather easier than shooting fish in a barrel.

Charles Paris noted that Ned English also looked different. Even back in Hornchurch days he had been completely grey, and yet for television he sported a glossy mane of chestnut hair. And his dark brown eyes now peered through round comedy tortoiseshell glasses.

Watching the repeat of *StarHunt* made Charles extremely cross. Is this what the theatre's come to? he fulminated into his whisky glass. Can't a production of one of Shakespeare's greatest plays get into the West End without this ridiculous publicity circus? And, even more pertinent, can't Ophelia be cast by the normal auditioning process, to reward some genuinely talented young person who has worked her way through drama school and the early dispiriting uncertainties of a professional career in the theatre? Rather than some jumped-up teenager from Essex whose Mum produced fond footage of her singing and dancing to the video camera at the age of two?

The thought brought Charles back to one of the enduring qualities of his profession – its unfairness. Like most actors, he reckoned that if talent were all, the hierarchy at the top of the theatrical tree would take a very different form. But it wasn't the most skilled actors who tended to get the breaks. It was often the ones who came with some publicity story attached, some special detail that brought them to the notice of the public. It didn't have to be much. Good looks were sometimes enough. Being in a relationship with someone more famous never hurt. And, of course, being born into a theatrical dynasty made you a shoo-in.

Charles Paris had lost count of the number of actors he had encountered who were more talented than the ones he'd seen become stars. And though he'd never admit it to anyone for fear of sounding as if he'd overdosed on sour grapes, he did actually include himself in that number. If only he'd had the breaks, Charles Paris's career could have been . . . But no, he must stop thinking like that. It wasn't helpful and was unlikely to improve his mood.

He thought back to a production of *Hamlet* he'd seen with his wife Frances not that long before. He couldn't remember exactly how long, and he wondered whether it was actually the last time they'd met. Must ring Frances, he reminded himself. Though they didn't cohabit, Charles liked to feel that there was a lot of warmth still between them.

The reason they had seen the production was that the actor playing Hamlet was the boyfriend of one of his wife's former pupils. (Frances was headmistress of a girls' school.) The girl – whatever her name was, he'd forgotten – was playing Ophelia. But what Charles remembered was being blown away by the young man's raw talent and the intelligence of his interpretation

of one of the best parts in world theatre. What was his name?
Something hyphenated . . . Oh yes, Sam Newton-Reid.

Charles remembered talking to the boy with his girlfriend
in the bar afterwards. The venue wasn't a particularly presti-
gious one, just an upstairs room in a pub in Battersea. And
despite the enthusiasm of the tiny audience, no newspaper
reviewers had seen the show. Sam and his girlfriend had tried
to get various influential people along . . . Charles seemed to
remember Tony Copeland's name being mentioned . . . but he
got the impression none of them had turned up.

So, despite having given one of the best performances of
Hamlet that Charles or Frances had seen for a long time, Sam
Newton-Reid looked to be going nowhere as a result of the
production. He hadn't got another acting job to go to and was
talking of a return to the job he'd had since leaving university
– working in telesales.

To Charles Paris that was just one more dispiriting story of
many in his profession. A talent like Sam Newton-Reid's would
probably shrivel up in disappointment while some primped-up
little madam from Essex would tread the West End stage as
Ophelia.

The grumpiness that *StarHunt* engendered in Charles was
another reason to hit the Bell's hard. So hard that he hadn't
even made it to bed and had been crumpled in an armchair
when the doorbell woke him at four in the morning.

TWO

C harles Paris hadn't had time to change his clothes. A quick brush through his hair and a toothpaste scrub at his teeth (which did little to diminish the arid metallic foulness inside his mouth), and he was on his way. He hoped the part Tibor Pincus had for him wasn't a clean-shaven one . . . though the girls in make-up usually had a razor around for such eventualities.

The journey out through the South London suburbs didn't do much to relieve the dry pounding in Charles's head, and when they turned off the A3, through some wiggly country roads, he began to feel distinctly sick.

But there was still a little wisp of excitement in him about the fact of being on location. There was something that got to an actor about working away from rehearsal room and theatre. Though all it often meant, particularly in the film industry, was hours of waiting around, the word 'location' still had a magic to it. Charles Paris even recalled a few romantic escapades which he had enjoyed in out-of-the-way hotels during filming. Illicit, of course, but then he'd been technically married to Frances for so long that almost all of his romantic escapades had been illicit. Besides, there's a casuistic expression current among married actors prone to straying. D.C.O.L. Which, of course, stands for 'Doesn't Count On Location'.

So, through his hangover, Charles was looking forward to the day. To dream of a sexual encounter was perhaps optimistic, but at least there was always location catering to look forward to. Again his memory brought back recollections of far too many bacon sandwiches consumed, still leaving room for lavish lunches, frequently eaten in converted double-decker buses. He looked out eagerly for the distinctive small village of trucks and trailers that indicated a shoot was in progress.

He was thus considerably disappointed when his minicab stopped in the deserted car park by the Newlands Corner Visitors' Centre alongside a single rented white van. 'Are you sure this is the right place?'

The driver shrugged. 'This is where I was told to take you. Pick-up time's seven this evening.' He thrust a card at Charles. 'If it's going to be very different, call this number.'

And the car was driving off almost before the back door had clicked shut. Abandoned, Charles Paris looked around at the early September morning. Though he'd left Hereford Road in darkness, the dawn had crept up unnoticed during the car-ride and it was now full daylight.

The scene the sun illuminated was a stunning one. Newlands Corner, near Guildford, commands splendid views over the Surrey hills, and is very popular with walkers and dog-owners. From the car park, tough grassland slopes downwards to the level of farmers' fields, beyond which can be seen the misty gentle curves of the North Downs. The terrain justifies its description as a 'beauty spot'. But that morning the landscape's charms were lost on Charles Paris; he was too preoccupied by his hangover to respond to the delights of nature.

There was no one sitting in the white van's driver or passenger seats, so he moved round the back. Only to discover that the doors were closed. No sign of life. He checked his watch. Five to six. He was actually early for his call . . . which had not always been the case in Charles Paris's theatrical career. But he would have expected more evidence of a film crew than this single van.

For a moment he felt a *frisson* of something almost like fear. Looking down into the darkly shadowed woodland, he recalled why Newlands Corner had rung a bell when Maurice Skellern had first mentioned the name. It was a significant location in the history of crime fiction, the place where Agatha Christie's car had been abandoned during her famous but still not completely explained disappearance in 1926. Just down the hill from the car park where he stood was the Silent Pool, near which her Morris Cowley was found.

The sun disappeared behind a cloud to add to Charles's

feeling of foreboding. And the hangover wasn't helping either. He stepped forward to the back doors of the white van, hand upraised to knock on them.

Then he had another thought and tried the handle. To his surprise it turned and the doors pulled outwards.

Some premonition had suggested to him that he'd find a body inside the van, but in fact he found two.

Both covered in a scrambled tartan rug. And very still.

But only for a moment. Then a head, disturbed by the sound and sunlight, poked up to look blearily at Charles. He saw the face of a girl in her early twenties with tousled dyed red hair. The way she clutched the rug to her neck suggested she didn't have a lot of clothes on.

Woken by her movement, the other body also came to life and peered, squinting, towards the open doors.

'Ah, Charles Paris,' said Tibor Pincus. Though his English was grammatically perfect, he still kept the thick accent from his native Budapest.

The famed director had not worn well. Most of his hair had gone and what remained was tufted by sleep into what looked like the crest of a battered seabird.

'Good morning,' said Charles, noticing with longing that amongst the horizontal empty wine bottles on the floor of the van stood upright a half-full litre of Teacher's whisky. Not his favourite brand, but that morning he was in no condition to be picky.

Tibor Pincus looked at his watch. 'On time, Charles. There has to be a first time for everything, eh? The cameraman is due at seven thirty and we need to have you ready for shooting by then.'

He nodded to the girl who, in one graceful movement, managed to stand up and drape the rug modestly about herself. Dexterously, she gathered up some clothes, including a pair of fluorescently pink knickers, and scuttled past Charles round to the front of the van.

The removal of the rug revealed Tibor Pincus to be lying on a grubby sleeping bag, unzipped and opened out like a kipper. He wore only a pair of checked boxer shorts, over which a pale belly dusted with white hair flopped precariously.

He tried to rise to his feet but had to ease himself up against the van's wall.

The director's hand moved painfully up to his head, and Charles found himself mirroring the gesture in sympathy.

'A few too many last night,' said Tibor Pincus.

'I know the feeling.'

Instinctively, the director's hand found the neck of the Teacher's bottle. In a single practised movement he unscrewed the top, brought the opening to his lips and took a grateful swig.

Reading something in Charles Paris's eyes, he then proffered the whisky towards the actor.

'Won't say no. Just a quick hair of the dog.'

Charles's swig was equally grateful.

'Ah yes, I remember,' said Tibor. 'Always had a taste for the booze, didn't you, Charles?'

'Well . . .' There was nothing more to say, really. It wasn't an observation with which he could argue. 'But I don't remember you as a drinker, Tibor.'

'No.' The director sighed, then took another long pull from the Teacher's bottle. 'You will find many things have changed about me, Charles.'

'Yes, thinking way back, when we worked together on that telly play in the eighties, there was quite a drinking culture among the cast. And you sat it out with your glass of orange juice. Very virtuous.'

'Probably less virtuous now, Charles. No, but as director I thought someone should remain in control. Also I loved the work I was doing and I didn't want to risk spoiling it by being less than a hundred per cent all of the time. Whereas with the work I'm doing now . . . huh, hard to spoil that.'

'What was the name of that actor, Tibor, who was in that play? You know, biggest piss artist in the theatre . . .?'

Tibor grinned. 'Charles Paris?'

'Ha bloody ha! Oh, what was his name? He had a success in a telly series that was big in the States, and then he went over to live there. Haven't heard much of him since.'

'You mean Portie,' said Tibor.

'That's right – Portie. Can't remember his real name, can

you?' Charles was finding more names escaped him nowadays.

Tibor Pincus shook his head. He couldn't remember either.

At least they did get bacon sandwiches. The girl, whom Tibor still hadn't introduced – or indeed spoken to since they had both been woken up – proved to be very efficient with a little Campingaz stove. She even had an appropriate supply of ketchup, mustard and – Charles's favourite – HP sauce.

When the two men, Tibor now dressed in denim shirt and jeans, were sitting on camping stools outside the open back door of the van with their sandwiches and mugs of dark brown tea (laced with a little Teacher's), Charles Paris thought it was the moment to ask about the filming project for which he had been summoned to Newlands Corner.

'Ah,' the director replied. 'Today, Charles, you are going to reconstruct the Battle of Naseby.'

'Oh yes? Me and whose army?'

'Nobody's army. It's just you, Charles.' The director gestured into the back of the van to some cellophane-shielded costumes. 'You are both the Roundheads and the Cavaliers.'

'No other actors involved?'

'No.'

Charles Paris's optimism, normally suppressed by uncompromising reality, did a little flutter like a baby quickening. Even the most cynical of actors retains that flicker of hope, the conviction their careers have yet to peak, that the big break is just around the corner. To be the only actor in a television play directed by the legendary Tibor Pincus, that was the kind of career-defining job that . . .

It didn't take long for the bubble to be pricked. 'What we're filming today,' Tibor went on, 'is filler stuff for one of those historical documentaries.' And he mentioned the name of the presenter Charles had ended up watching in Hereford Road the previous night.

'The one with big breasts?'

The director nodded. 'The one with big breasts, yes. She's doing a series on the Civil War. And you, Charles, are going to be all the soldiers on both sides in the Battle of Naseby.'

'Is this one of these computer-generated things, where I'll

be cloned and made to look like thousands of versions of myself?' Though not strong on the details, Charles knew that a lot of work on television films was now done post-production. And that a lot of directors had a lot more fun fiddling with technical effects in the editing suite than they did dealing with the inconvenience of actors. (He also remembered a wistful line he had heard quoted from the writer Alan Plater: 'When I started in television, "post-production" was going down the pub.')

But Charles Paris was not about to become a component in a sequence of computer generated imagery. 'No, no,' said Tibor Pincus. 'There will just be one of you, no technical trickery. I will shoot you in a variety of close-ups – a boot here, a bit of a breastplate there, your gauntleted hand gripping a pike, swords scraping against each other . . . that kind of thing. Then at the end of the day we'll do lots of shots of you dying.'

'Right.'

'Just falling over, throwing your hands up in the air, you know. We'll do that in both Roundhead and Cavalier costumes.' Tibor picked up the ketchup bottle on the camping table between them. 'We'll use a lot of this.'

Charles nodded. 'OK, fine.' He looked out from their vantage point over the comforting undulations of the Surrey hills. 'From my recollection of history,' he said, 'the Battle of Naseby was fought in open fields in Northamptonshire. Very flat open fields.'

'So . . .?'

'Well, I can't help noticing that, however you might wish to describe this landscape, the one adjective you wouldn't use is "flat".'

The Hungarian shrugged. 'Charles, the programme is being made by a production company based in London. They're not going to pay to send a crew out to Northamptonshire. They want a location that's accessible inside a day, with no overnight expenses.'

'But you still chose to stay overnight.'

'That was for personal reasons.' Tibor caught the eye of the girl who had just joined them with Charles's costume (he was going to be the New Model Army first, rather than the Royalists). The girl winked back.

Charles Paris was impressed. He hoped he would demonstrate the same physical robustness when he was Tibor Pincus's age. The idea of continuing to live after he had lost the capacity to make love didn't hold much appeal for Charles. And it had been a while, he reminded himself. Maybe it'd never happen again. Maybe he'd already made love to his last woman. Oh dear, another thing to worry about.

The director gestured across the vista in front of him. 'It doesn't matter where we shoot this stuff. So the Battle of Naseby was fought on flat terrain and here we're on hilly terrain? Makes no difference. Everything's going to be shot in such tight close-up we could be filming it in a branch of Tesco's.'

'It's funny,' Charles mused, 'I'd never really thought about how they get the footage for these documentaries. I imagined they'd do it all on the cheap. But it seems that they do have quite high production values.'

'Where are the high production values?' asked a bewildered Tibor.

'Well, I mean, getting a director of your stature . . . It shows they really care what the footage looks like.'

'Oh yes?'

'A director like you can't come cheap.'

Tibor Pincus looked at him bleakly. Most of the colour had been washed out of his watery blue eyes. 'You wouldn't believe how cheap I come these days, Charles.'

'But surely, someone with your track record . . .'

'Who cares about my track record? You have to remember, television is now run by twelve year olds fresh out of Media Studies courses. What do they know about the past? What do they care about the past? Most of the people I used to work with have now retired. And the few who are left are now so high up the management structure they don't even return my calls. It's been decades since anyone would give me a proper job.

'Do you think I'd be reconstructing the English Civil War with one actor if I had any alternative? Making television by the yard. The shots of you will be intercut with the odd castle ruin, stained glass window, faded document, out-of-focus sparkling water, sunlight through ferns. Visual pap, chewing gum for the eyes.' The director shrugged. 'But it's work, Charles, and the only work I can get these days.'

'Ah.' There was a silence, then Charles said, 'Well, thank you for booking me for today, Tibor.'

'My pleasure. Why, is this the only work you can get too?'

'Pretty much.'

At that moment a Range Rover drove up to the van and the cameraman got out. He was a lugubrious soul who did as Tibor Pincus told him, talking minimally, offering no suggestions, just getting on with the job for which he was being paid.

And that was it. The other film-set personnel Charles had been expecting didn't appear. The girl whose name he still hadn't been given – and wasn't volunteered – did everything that the cameraman didn't. She got Charles into his costume, did his make-up and acted as PA to Tibor, making a shot list as he filmed bits of their one actor. She also cooked a very good lunch on the Campingaz stove. Under the disapproving scrutiny of the cameraman, director and actor washed the food down with copious draughts of Teacher's. (The first bottle had been long finished, but Tibor had a crate of them in the back of the van.)

When it came to the point of filming his various deaths at the end of the day, particularly given the gradient of the Newlands Corner hill, Charles Paris didn't have any problem with falling down a lot.

THREE

It was a night of many vows. As Charles Paris tossed about on his bed at Hereford Road, his body aching – and not just from the bruises he had suffered at Newlands Corner – he swore that he would finally give up the booze. The harm it must be doing to his liver, the harm it had already done to his liver, didn't bear contemplating. Not just the liver, either. The papers were always full of gloomy prognostications about the long-term damage excessive drinking could do. Heart attacks, strokes, throat cancer . . . ugh.

And think of the money he'd save if he gave up.

Not just that. Think of the self-respect he'd regain. It was still possible to turn his life around, he tried to convince himself. He was only in his late fifties, after all. What career breaks might lie ahead for a completely sober Charles Paris?

He might even get back into a permanent cohabiting relationship with his estranged wife Frances. After all, the booze was one of the main things she had against him. Well, that and his tendency to become over-involved with young actresses (he refused to think of them as 'actors' if he was going to bed with them). Anyway, a sober Charles Paris was less likely to get involved with young actresses. It was the breakdown of inhibition caused by alcohol which had frequently led him into unsuitable beds, late-night drinking sessions after performances, First Night parties, that kind of thing. A sober Charles Paris might be a more virtuous Charles Paris. And it wasn't as if he'd ever stopped loving Frances.

Yes, total abstinence was the only possible way forward.

But even as he had this thought, he realized how much of his social life revolved around drinking. Total abstinence was a bit extreme . . . puritanical . . . po-faced, even. One thing he'd never wanted to be was a party-pooper. If he cut out the whisky . . . restricted himself to the occasional pint . . . the odd glass of wine . . .? He didn't want to become a self-righteous prig about the whole business. Not a humourless Alcoholics Anonymous type, one of those people of whom it could be said: 'Anyone who breaks a habit usually frames the pieces.'

But then he changed position in bed and felt the tectonic plates of the hangover shifting in his head. Jagged shards of brain ground against each other. The pain was very physical, very local. He could have touched exactly where it hurt, all the places where it hurt.

No, total abstinence was the only possible solution.

He drank water to rehydrate his powdered brain cells. Then round six o'clock, just as the rosy fingers of dawn were beginning to tickle the Westbourne Grove area, he succumbed and downed what was left in the Bell's bottle. Just so's he could get a little sleep.

It was a portentous moment, he knew it. His last ever drink of Bell's. He would never buy another bottle. Never again would he experience the sensation of twisting the metal cap free with his fingers. Never again would he taste that welcome burning on his tongue, the warmth as it slipped down his throat. He had made a vow. No more Bell's. No more Teacher's. No more whisky of any kind. For ever and ever. Amen.

Feeling almost impossibly virtuous, Charles Paris slipped into an uneasy sleep.

He was woken at ten thirty-five by the telephone.

For a moment he couldn't decide whether it was his landline or his mobile. Not that it made a great deal of difference. He couldn't see either in the chaos of clothes, bedding, books and old copies of *The Times* that littered his floor.

Eventually, he uncovered the mobile. The moment he picked it up the ringing stopped.

Now, Charles Paris wasn't very good with mobiles. He'd resisted owning one for as long as possible. But finally, the disappearance of phone booths from the high street and, on the rare occasions when he was in work, the habit of stage managers sending out rehearsal calls by text made him realize that he had to succumb to the new technology.

But even then Charles only wanted a mobile to make and

receive phone calls. The other potentialities of the instrument – its ability to take photographs, receive emails and, for all he knew, make fresh pasta – were of no interest to him. He heard people talking about apps, but he had no idea what an app was. He had, however, managed to find out how to access the Call Log and from this he discovered that the person who had woken him was Maurice Skellern.

Charles needed to assemble himself slightly before he actually conversed with anyone. He looked wistfully at the bottle of Bell's, but it remained resolutely empty. He filled a large glass of water at the tiny sink in his tiny kitchen and downed as much of it as he could before he started choking.

He scrabbled through the contents of his bathroom cabinet in search of paracetamol, but found only a fully-popped bubble sheet. Have to do some shopping soon, he thought. For paracetamol. And, of course, for a bottle of whisky, without which he wouldn't need the paracetamol.

Except he wasn't going to buy any more whisky, was he? Ever again.

He tried unsuccessfully to drink a little more water before he rang back.

'Maurice Skellern Artistes.'

'Maurice, it's Charles. Sorry, I heard your call ringing just as I was coming back through the door.' How easily, how instinctively the untruth slipped out.

'Ah, Charles. Well, who's the popular boy then?'

'Presumably your *wunderkind* Edgar. As I've mentioned a few times before, Maurice, I don't like hearing about your other—'

'No, no, I wasn't ringing about Edgar. I was ringing about you, Charles.'

'Really?'

'Yes, two enquiries about you in the same week. That has to be some kind of record, doesn't it?'

'What is it this—?'

'How did the filming with Tibor go yesterday?'

'Fine. It turned out to be just close-up shots of me representing the Battle of Naseby. Wallpaper for some historical documentary.'

'Oh yes, I knew that.'

If you knew it, then why the hell didn't you mention it to me, thought Charles. Instead of letting me think I had a part in some major drama. But it wasn't worth saying out loud. There were a lot of things it just wasn't worth saying to Maurice.

'I hear,' the agent went on, 'that Tibor Pincus has got a bit of a drink problem these days. Not so good in the afternoon, eh?'

'I didn't see any sign of it,' Charles lied. 'Anyway, what's the new enquiry?'

'Ned English.'

'Really? Name from the past.'

'Yes, totally buried in the mire of obscurity I'd have said. Though his profile has increased recently with this new telly he's doing.'

'*StarHunt.*'

'Very good, Charles. I don't normally expect you to be so up to date with all the new shows.'

'Oh, I try to keep abreast,' came the nonchalant reply. Wouldn't do to mention that he hadn't heard of *StarHunt* until randomly catching a repeat a couple of nights before.

'Well, Ned wants to talk to you.'

'Oh. About this *Hamlet* he's doing?' Why was it no actor could hear of the word 'Hamlet' without that little irrational surge of excitement, that thought: *Have they finally seen the errors of their ways? Are they finally going to offer me the opportunity to show that I could be the defining Hamlet of my generation?* A bit old for the part maybe, Charles reassured himself, but I can play younger. After all, the famous French tragedienne Sarah Bernhardt played Hamlet at the age of fifty-five. And she was a woman. And she had a wooden leg.

'Well, I suppose it might be,' Maurice Skellern conceded.

'Come on, I can't imagine there's much else Ned's doing at the moment.'

'Oh, you never know. Now he's a telly face he'll be getting invited on to all kinds of tatty panel shows. Maybe he wants to talk to you about appearing as his gardener in one of those "Guess Which is the Real One" quizzes.'

'Did he say that's what it was?'

'No.'

'Then did he say it was for the *Hamlet*?'

'No.'

'Oh.'

'What he did say was that he'd like to meet you for lunch today at the Ivy.'

'Really?' Charles was impressed. 'I'll just check my diary to see if I'm—'

'Don't bother with that,' said his agent. 'As I told Ned, one thing never changes about Charles Paris – he's always free.'

He had been to the Ivy before, but rarely. And that had been a while ago, before it became the canteen for the top people in the entertainment business.

Charles was shown to Ned English's table. In spite of the glossy chestnut hair, the director's face looked old and worried. During their conversation, his dark brown eyes behind the round tortoiseshell glasses kept darting round the restaurant, his hand ever ready to wave at some celebrity who might recognize him.

He also, in the voguish way which still always rather surprised Charles, greeted his guest in an enveloping bear hug.

Ned's manner to the bright young waiters was a bit too studiedly casual, as if their acquaintance went back years rather than the few months of his recent television fame. All in all, he was giving a very bad impression of a person who was entirely at ease in his environment.

Charles Paris's resolve not to have another drink that day lasted until Ned English, with the waiter hovering at his shoulder, demanded, 'So what'll you have as an aperitif?'

His body craved an extremely large scotch on the rocks, but noticing that Ned was drinking a *kir royale*, Charles asked for one of those. Champagne and cassis was, after all, almost a soft drink. Nothing with bubbles in it, he reasoned, could really be regarded as alcoholic. He felt virtuous for avoiding the spirits.

And he continued to feel virtuous as he and Ned worked through a bottle of Sauvignon Blanc and a Rioja Reserva during the meal.

Their conversation began with a recap of what each had been doing during the twenty-seven years since they'd last met. Ned English did most of the talking. Charles's life didn't really seem to have changed a lot over that time. As ever, there had been long periods of 'resting', interrupted by occasional flurries of work. His marriage to Frances retained its continuity of rapprochements and partings. And, except for his involvement in solving the odd murder (which he wasn't going to talk about), there was not a lot to tell.

As Ned burbled on about his doings, Charles Paris suspected that the director didn't really have a lot to tell either. But somehow in the intervening twenty-seven years he had transformed himself from *enfant terrible* to 'a safe pair of hands'. Most of his recent work had been directing touring versions of reliable old plays with celebrity leads. And all of them had been done for Tony Copeland's production company. Charles didn't ask the question as to why Ned English had got the high-profile job of directing the *StarHunt Hamlet*, but he felt fairly sure it had something to do with his history of work with Tony Copeland. Also, having seen the television show, he knew why the producer wanted such a pliable punchbag as his sidekick.

Some fifteen years seemed to have been edited out of the CV that Ned presented to Charles. Of the time between their last meeting in Hornchurch and when he had started working for Tony Copeland no mention at all was made. And after a bit of big name-dropping about the people he'd worked with on his touring productions, Ned English's talk focused exclusively on *StarHunt*.

Charles had found during his career that there were two sorts of directors – the ones who relished the limelight (and covertly thought that they could do the acting bit better than their actors), and those who just got on with the job, content to remain in the background. He infinitely preferred working with the second kind. And would indeed previously have put Ned English into that category. But the lure of the television camera was powerful. As his behaviour on *StarHunt* made clear, Ned had always wanted to be a 'personality'.

'It is quite boring, actually, Charles, being "on show" all

the time,' he complained (though clearly loving every minute of it). 'I can't even go down to the supermarket without someone starting an argument with me about one of the contestants who got eliminated in the previous night's show. And you wouldn't believe the number of tweets I get on a daily basis.'

Charles, whose knowledge of what a tweet was might not have passed close scrutiny, agreed that he probably wouldn't.

'And then, of course, the number of calls I get for me to do media stuff . . . well, you just wouldn't believe it. I've had to get a new ex-directory landline . . . and I've engaged a PR company to handle all that side. Mangetout Creative . . . do you know them?'

'No,' said Charles.

'So who handles yours?'

'My what?'

'Well, your personal . . . No, no, it wouldn't apply to you, of course. Anyway, believe me, the whole thing's an absolute nightmare.'

'Yes.'

'Though it's not without its compensations,' Ned English added slyly.

'Oh?'

'Women are very attracted to men who're on television.'

'Really?'

'Oh yes,' said Ned with a roguish wink. 'Particularly young women. You'd be surprised how many dishy young female actors –' he had got his political correctness right – 'are happy to spend the time of day – not to mention the time of night – with someone who's a judge on *StarHunt*.'

'Good for you. When we were in Hornchurch – have I got this right – you were married, weren't you?'

'Oh, that didn't last,' came the airy reply. 'You still with . . .?'

'Frances,' Charles supplied.

'Yes. You two still together?'

'Well . . .'

But he didn't get a chance to describe his strangely semi-detached relationship with Frances, as the director ploughed on smugly: 'I am currently squiring round London a female actor who's younger than my daughter.'

'Really?'

'The sex is just amazing.'

'Is it?' Ned was clearly ready to give him more detail, but Charles didn't think he could stand it. He'd nearly finished his Chicken Paillard with Tomato and Mint Chimichurri, and Ned still hadn't mentioned the real reason for their lunch. 'I did actually wonder what you wanted to talk to me about . . .?'

'But, Charles, isn't it wonderful for two old chums just to get together for old time's sake?'

'Well, yes, it is. Wonderful. Splendid. But, you know, after twenty-seven years . . . I mean, it's very nice of you to take me out for lunch . . .' A terrible shadow crossed over Charles Paris's mind. He was, as ever, hideously overdrawn and on the run from the taxman. 'I mean, that is, I assume this is on you . . .?'

'No, it's not on me.' Oh shit, thought Charles. 'It's on Tony Copeland Productions.'

The 'Phew' that formed in Charles's mind was almost audible.

'The fact is, old boy . . .' Since when had the *enfant terrible* of English theatre been calling people 'old boy' like some superannuated actor/manager? It'd be 'laddie' next. 'The fact is that it was in connection with this production of *Hamlet* that I wanted to talk to you. You know, the *StarHunt* one which—'

'I know the one you mean.'

'You wouldn't believe the amount of flouncing backstage that goes on with that show. I mean, when we rejected that Bangladeshi girl Anjali, well, the story was leaked to the tabloids that . . .' And Ned English was off again into anecdotage about his fame as a television star.

As their conversation moved further and further away from potential work for Charles Paris, his hopes slowly deflated. Reality had caught up sufficiently for him to realize he wasn't going to be offered Hamlet. But Claudius was surely a possibility . . .? Or Polonius . . .? Of course, Charles wasn't really old enough for the part, but he could 'age up'.

As Ned English blethered on, though, his hopes moved down through the dramatis personae. Fortinbras . . .?

Osric . . .? Second Gravedigger . . .? Reynaldo, Servant to Polonius . . .? A character that didn't even have a name . . .? A Captain . . .? Sailor . . .? Attendant . . .?

This mournful downward spiral was interrupted by his hearing Ned say, '. . . so I'd like you to double the Ghost and First Gravedigger.'

'The Ghost? The Ghost of Hamlet's Father?'

'Yes.'

'And the First Gravedigger?'

'Yes.'

Charles Paris's spirits lifted. All right, it wasn't Claudius or Polonius. But the Ghost and the First Gravedigger were both decent roles. Also, he'd have to use different accents for the two of them, and there's nothing actors like more than demonstrating their versatility.

No, the Ghost of Hamlet's Father and the First Gravedigger were good parts. Not the best parts, which, of course, involve gibbering. But the only character who gets to gibber in *Hamlet* is Ophelia in the Mad Scene. It is a fact that all actors love gibbering parts. Caliban, the deformed slave, is so much more fun to play than Prospero, the po-faced voice of authority. As well as dragging various malfunctioning limbs around the stage, with Caliban you can give him a kind of deformed voice as well – a wonderful gibbering opportunity. Even Edgar in *King Lear*, that most dull and upright of heroes, gets a chance to gibber when he's disguised as Poor Tom o' Bedlam. There's nothing actors like better than being deformed and gibbering on stage. 'I want to be deformed and gibber!' they cry. It's a hell of a lot more fun playing Smike than Nicholas Nickleby. There are even Oscars in it. 'Cast me in *My Left Foot*, please!' 'Let me be in *Rain Man*!' Daniel Day Lewis and Dustin Hoffman have done very well out of gibbering. And then again, coming back to basics, playing people who gibber is so much easier than playing real people. 'Please,' is the actor's nightly prayer, 'whatever I'm cast in next, may it be someone who gibbers!'

All right, Charles Paris reassured himself, the Ghost of Hamlet's Father and the First Gravedigger don't get to gibber, but they're still a nice doubling opportunity. A very attractive proposition.

'So,' asked Charles tentatively, 'are you offering me the parts, Ned?'

'Pretty much. I mean, I have to run all the casting past Tony . . .'

'And is he likely to raise any objections?'

'Oh, he'll do the usual producer's thing of wanting starrier names . . .'

'Ah.'

'. . . but I think I can win him round on that.'

'Good.'

'The thing is, when you've got leads who are not very experienced, not in stage work, anyway—'

'Oh, by the way, you haven't told me the most important thing about the production. Who is playing Hamlet?'

Ned English looked elaborately around the room, scrutinized the table cloth as if checking it for hidden microphones and leant across towards Charles. 'Now I shouldn't be telling you this. It's embargoed till the night of the *StarHunt* final, but our Hamlet will be . . . no less a person than . . .' Ned had certainly mastered the reality show trick of holding a very long pause before a revelation; he was only lacking the dramatic build-up music '. . . Jared Root.'

'Ah,' said Charles profoundly, as if the name meant a light to him. 'Jared Root, the . . . er . . .'

'The winner of last year's *Top Pop*.'

The programme's name was vaguely familiar. 'But wasn't that a music contest?'

Ned English nodded excitedly. 'Yes. And given Jared Root's profile with the teen audience, his presence is going to mean lots of lovely young bums on seats.'

'So,' asked Charles, a little bewildered, 'Hamlet is going to be played by a singer?'

Another excited nod.

'Couldn't they get an actor?'

'Ah now, Charles, this is where it gets really good. It turns out that Jared Root is not just a singer. He came out of Italia Conti.'

'The stage school?'

'Yes. So it means he can act as well as sing!'

'Really?'

'Yes. He played Badger in *Toad of Toad Hall* in his final year!'

'Wouldn't you say it was a bit of a jump from Badger to Hamlet?'

'Not with me directing, Charles, no. But the thing is, because Jared Root is not very experienced . . . and because our Ophelia is unlikely to be very experienced either . . .'

Charles thought back to what he had seen of the aspirants on *StarHunt*. 'You can say that again.'

'. . . I want to surround them with actors who are absolutely rock solid.'

'Oh.' Charles Paris smiled, recognizing that he'd just been paid a compliment.

'And if Tony Copeland argues about my casting, I'll tell him: I have gone, not necessarily for the best actors for the roles, but ones who I know won't cause any trouble during the production.'

'Ah.' Charles Paris stopped smiling, recognizing that the compliment he'd recently been paid had now been considerably diluted.

'I'm going to have my hands full,' Ned English went on, 'with two comparative amateurs in the leading roles, so I have to make sure I surround them with solid, biddable professionals.'

'Solid' and 'biddable' were not the two adjectives Charles would have chosen to be carved on the tombstone of his career, but on the other hand he had just been offered some work. Two nice parts. He resolved to be exactly as solid and biddable as Ned English required.

When, at the end of their meal, the waiter asked if they would like any *digestif*, Ned said they ought to have something to celebrate what he hoped would be a renewal of their working relationship.

Charles didn't demur. Ned had an Armagnac, Charles a Laphroaig malt whisky.

And on his way back to Hereford Road, he stopped at a convenience store in Westbourne Grove for a bottle of Bell's. To continue celebrating.

FOUR

'**A**nd the set, as you can see from this model,' said Ned English, 'is kind of like the interior of a cranium.'

Oh God. Charles winced inwardly, remembering the productions with which the director had first made his name. *He's not going to set the whole thing inside Yorick's skull, is he?* Years before, Charles Paris had actually taken part in another production set in a cranium. *The Tempest*, directed by someone who, as the rehearsal unwound, revealed himself to be a complete loony. As ever, Charles could remember the notice he'd received for his very small contribution to the production. 'Even Charles Paris, as the Shipmaster, looked as if he'd rather be acting in another play entirely. And he had my sympathy.' – *Shropshire Star*.

'Now,' the director went on, 'I'll hand over to our designer to have a few words about how the set'll work.'

Charles Paris remained at the back of the cast as they crowded round for a look at the neatly carved cardboard set model. It was the first day of rehearsal for the Tony Copeland Productions' *Hamlet*. The rehearsal room was in an old barracks in Kilburn, which had ceased to be a military building in a recent round of defence cuts and was awaiting redevelopment. Before the cast arrived, the stage management team had marked out the dimensions of the set with coloured tape on the wooden floor. In the centre of the space they had set up a large table surrounded by chairs for the read-through. Against the wall was a smaller table with a tall water heater, tins of coffee powder, tea bags, biscuits and all the other necessities of the rehearsal period.

The designer's explanation of his set was, to Charles's mind, somewhat abstruse. He seemed to have got overexcited by the idea of reproducing the human skull and kept on about how closely what he was building would mirror the real thing. Very proud of his knowledge of human anatomy, the designer showed how the giant interior of the cranium would be built up in sections matching the bones of a human skull. There would be a frontal bone, two parietal bones, and two temporal bones. And the main entrance at the back of the stage would correspond with the gap in the occipital bone through which the vertebral column is connected to the cranial cavity.

All of this talk sounded warning bells for Charles. His main concern about a set was not how closely it corresponded to what it referenced but how easy it was to get on and off. And how likely or unlikely it was to fall down.

'The thing is,' Ned English picked up, cutting through the hubbub of comments about the model, 'that my reading of *Hamlet* is going to be based on one line that the Prince himself says. *"For there is nothing either good or bad but thinking makes it so."'*

Oh no, thought Charles Paris. It's going to be set inside Hamlet's skull, not Yorick's.

'Which is why,' said the director, 'the action of the play is going to be set inside Hamlet's skull.'

Ye gods!

'Anyway,' Ned continued, 'let's all sit down and get started on this read-through.'

The cast did as instructed. Charles Paris looked around the table. So far as he could remember, he had not worked with any of the other actors before. There were a couple of faces familiar from the telly, including Katrina Selsey, the Essex girl with blonde hair, blue eyes framed with mascaraed false lashes and teeth of a whiteness not on God's colour chart, who had come through to triumph in *StarHunt* and won the coveted role of Ophelia. Sitting next to her was a smart-suited young woman to whom the new star chatted continuously. Charles couldn't imagine what part in *Hamlet* the other girl might be playing. Surely she was too young for Gertrude. The Player Queen perhaps . . .? Though there was something about her manner that didn't make her look like an actress. (*Oops!* Charles reprimanded himself. *Actor!*) She also kept handing out business cards to anyone who came near her.

Charles couldn't help noticing how much make-up Katrina Selsey and the girl beside her were wearing. He felt an awful old fogey for being so aware of it. Having grown up through the sixties, Charles had a predilection for unenhanced female beauty – Frances had very rarely worn any make-up during the early, happy years of their marriage. But now young teenagers wouldn't leave the house without levels of face-painting as thick as those used in nineteenth-century opera. He couldn't help being reminded of a line he'd had to read in a Radio Four programme about John Evelyn. On the eleventh of May 1654, the great diarist had written: 'I now observed how the women began to paint themselves, formerly a most ignominious thing and us'd only by prostitutes.' Charles knew that his own views on make-up, if articulated, would sound equally reactionary. So he must make damn sure he never articulated them. Oh dear, in the brave new world he now inhabited, there were so many things he didn't dare say out loud.

Glancing round at the assembled cast, Charles reminded himself that *Hamlet* wasn't much of a play for an actor with a roving eye. Gertrude, Ophelia, the Player Queen (and that part was sometimes voguishly played by a boy). Add in the occasional Court Lady and that was it so far as potential sexual encounters were concerned. Unless, of course, you were gay. Yes, with all those male roles, *Hamlet* could be a very promising play if you were gay.

Mind you, one of the Assistant Stage Managers, who'd been introduced as Milly Henryson, was very pretty. Long black hair swept back into a hair tie and lovely dark-blue eyes. But terribly young. First job out of drama school perhaps. As Charles eyed her covertly, he had a nagging feeling he'd met her somewhere. But he couldn't think where. Still, with looks like that she might go far in the theatre. Assuming she could act. Actually, with looks like that, even assuming she couldn't act.

Charles hardly even rebuked himself for thinking so immediately about sex, but old habits died hard. He was meeting for the first time a group of people with whom he could well be spending the next six months. Or even longer. Checking out the available women was a simple knee-jerk reaction.

Except, of course, who could say whether they were actually available? And, he reminded himself, the new squeaky

clean Charles Paris was intending to get back with his wife,
wasn't he? As well as give up the booze. Something which
he hadn't quite managed to do yet. Which reminded him, he
really must ring Frances. How long was it since they had last
spoken? Weeks, certainly. Possibly even months. Must ring
Frances.

Even as he had the thought, he found himself smiling at
the woman opposite. Late forties, possibly early fifties, hair
dyed copper-coloured, she must be playing Gertrude. Very
attractive, though. Charles was pleased to see that she smiled
back at him. Mind you, he reminded himself, actresses – no,
female actors, dammit – smile at anyone.

Another of the ASMs came across to him. Good-looking
boy, dark-haired, thin, nervous, probably about twenty. 'Just
wanted to check we've got the right mobile number for you.'

Charles looked at the proffered list. 'Yes, that's right. And,
sorry, your name is . . .?'

'Will Portlock.'

'ASMing, are you?'

'Yes. But I'm also playing Second Gravedigger.'

'Oh, great, we'll have our scene together then. Trying to
screw laughs out of some of the worst puns in the whole of
English literature.'

'Yes.' The boy grinned shyly but proudly. 'I'm also understudying Hamlet.'

'Wow. Congratulations.'

'Mm. Awful position, really, isn't it? Because, of course,
I'd feel terrible if anything were to happen to Jared, but . . .'

Charles Paris grinned. He'd done the job often enough to
know about the conflicts of ambitions and fantasies which the
understudy cannot keep out of his mind. He was about to offer
words of encouragement to Will Portlock, but was interrupted
by the Stage Manager announcing that the read-through was
starting.

'Right,' said Ned English when everyone was seated round
the table, 'let's get this show on the road.'

There was a tremor in his voice and a sheen of sweat on
his brow. Charles hoped that the chestnut hair dye wasn't about
to run.

But the tell-tale signs made him realize just how much on edge Ned English was. The director kept looking cautiously towards Tony Copeland, who was present with a male sidekick, a man who'd been introduced simply as 'Doug Haye, from Tony Copeland Productions', without any explanation as to what his role was in the business. Haye was a stocky, pugnacious-looking man with a shaved head and features that ran together like a melted candle. During the entire morning of the read-through Charles Paris did not hear him speak once.

Tony Copeland himself invariably dressed in a pinstriped suit and wore a tie. His dark hair was short with a neat parting. Rimless glasses sat on a face which looked almost bland. But he wore an unmistakable aura of power. No wonder Ned English was afraid of him.

The director also seemed very nervous of Jared Root and Katrina Selsey. The penny dropped for Charles. He wasn't the only 'solid, biddable' actor who'd been drafted into the production. That was why Charles hadn't recognized many of the other actors. Ned English had cast 'old mates', people he'd worked with before. He was preparing for possible tantrums and flouncing from his Hamlet and Ophelia, so wanted to be certain he wouldn't get any temperament from the rest of the cast.

There also might well have been a financial reason for Ned's selection of actors. The deal Maurice Skellern had agreed with Tony Copeland Productions for Charles Paris's services had not been lavish, given that the four-week regional tour of *Hamlet* was going to be followed by – or at least there was an option clause in the contract for it to be followed by – a minimum of three months in the West End. Maybe the rest of the cast were employed on comparably meagre terms.

If that were the case, there was an obvious and not very pleasing corollary. Jared Root and Katrina Selsey must be being paid a great deal, which was the reason why money was being saved on the rest of the budget. Charles Paris was long accustomed to being in shows whose stars had been paid infinitely more than he was (and had sometimes also been on a percentage of box office receipts as well), but they had at least been genuine stars. The winners of *Top Pop* and *StarHunt* could hardly be placed in that category. They were media mushrooms which had sprung up overnight, and might equally quickly shrivel and die.

'All right,' Ned English continued, the tremor still in his voice. 'Some of you I'm sure have met each other already, but just so's everyone knows each other, let's go round the table and each identify ourselves and what our role is in this production of *Hamlet*. Well, I'll start. In case you don't know – or haven't worked it out – I'm Ned English and I have the great honour of directing this Tony Copeland production. OK, let's go clockwise round the table.'

Which they did. Some of the actors tried to make jokes and get laughs on their introductions. Charles didn't. He just said, 'I'm Charles Paris – doubling the Ghost of Hamlet's Father and First Gravedigger.'

He was interested when the dishy woman opposite announced that her name was Geraldine Romelle. And yes, he'd been right, she was playing Gertrude.

The other introduction of which he took particular note was for the suited young woman next to the production's Ophelia. 'I'm Peri Maitland from Pridmore Baines. I'm Katrina Selsey's Personal Manager.'

This was something new in Charles Paris's experience of read-throughs. The expression on Ned English's face suggested that the presence of a Personal Manager at such an event was something new to him too. But at least it explained why the girl didn't look like an actress. And why she kept handing round business cards.

'It's just,' said Katrina Selsey, 'since winning *StarHunt* I've had so much media attention, I never go anywhere without Peri.'

'I've got a Personal Manager too,' interposed Jared Root, a gym-toned, bushy-eyebrowed young man who looked as if he probably needed to shave five times a day. 'I just didn't think it was appropriate to bring him to a read-through.'

The moment passed, but Jared's remark had undoubtedly been a put-down and potentially a sign of conflicts to come. If the two new stars were going to be constantly at odds about which was the more famous, the ensuing weeks could be incident-full. Charles noticed covert looks and raised eyebrows being exchanged between the 'solid, biddable' actors who made up the rest of the cast.

After the introductions, Ned English made an uneasy, repetitive little speech about his 'vision' of *Hamlet*. Basically, it kept coming back to what he'd said earlier, that for him the key line was: '*There is nothing good or bad but thinking makes it so.*'

'The "rotten" state of Denmark,' he insisted, "is a dystopia viewed through the jaundiced eye of Hamlet. All the action of the play is seen through Hamlet's eyes.'

Charles Paris's view was that this thesis was arguable, but he was prepared to wait and see how it worked in practice. He wasn't too worried. He had been in too many productions where the director's 'vision' had been lost before the second week of rehearsal and they'd ended up doing a pretty conventional presentation of the text.

Ned then handed over to Tony Copeland, with a deference which bordered on toadyism, to say a few words from the producer's point of view.

Tony welcomed everyone, saying that he did know a few of those present from other Tony Copeland Productions' shows (hardly surprising, given the fact Ned English worked almost exclusively for the company and favoured the 'old mates' approach to casting). The producer outlined the details of the tour (which those present who had read their contracts, a number that did not include Charles Paris, knew already). *Hamlet* would open at Marlborough's Grand Theatre on a Wednesday and play there till the Saturday of the following week. The show would then do single weeks in Malvern, Wilmslow and Newcastle before – 'barring accidents' – opening after another week of rehearsal and previews at the Richardson Theatre in London's West End.

Tony Copeland announced that he was 'very excited' about the production, and expressed his laudable ambition that it would get a younger demographic into the West End theatre audience. The publicity generated by *StarHunt*, not to mention *Top Pop*, would, he opined, guarantee the show's success.

His presentation style was lacklustre, almost dull. The

mastery of the acerbic one-liner which he demonstrated on
StarHunt had been replaced by a manner that was nearly
self-effacing.

At the end of his routine he introduced the Company
Manager, a motherly woman employed by Tony Copeland
Productions. She went through a few practical details, mostly
about accommodation for the tour, and handed over to the
Stage Manager, who gave the company information about
rehearsal calls and that kind of thing.

'Right,' said Ned English at the end of this litany, 'let's get
reading. From now on, we'll give ourselves up to the magic
of the Bard.'

Charles Paris winced inwardly. The director's words had
sounded impossibly twee.

But they had nonetheless signalled the start of the reading.
The cast all opened their specially printed copies of the script
(which had been cut quite considerably – a full-length version
of *Hamlet* can easily last over four hours, which might put a
strain on the attention span of the remote-control-zapping
'younger demographic' Tony Copeland was trying to attract).

The actor playing Bernardo (as well as Osric later in the
play) was a young man who, in the round-the-table introductions, had announced himself as 'Dennis Demetriades'. His
Greek heritage showed in his black hair and dark shadow. On
the point of his chin was a perfect triangle of beard; above
his lips were two thinner, but equally well-trimmed triangles
of moustache.

'*Who's there?*' he started, but was quickly interrupted by
Ned English.

'Sorry, hadn't started the watch.' The director nodded to
Milly Henryson, one of whose responsibilities as Assistant
Stage Manager was clearly the stopwatch. She clicked the
relevant button. Again Dennis Demetriades asked, '*Who's
there?*', and this time Shakespeare's famous enquiry into identity and dithering began.

The read-through got off to a very strong start. Though
Charles Paris as the Ghost appeared in the opening scene, his
character did not actually speak, so he was able to appreciate
the work of the other actors. Ned English may have done his

casting from a repertoire of 'old mates', but at least his old mates knew how to speak verse. As ever, Charles found himself caught up and energized by the rhythms of Shakespeare's lines. He luxuriated in the power of the language.

All went fine until the second scene when, at the end of Claudius's conversation with Laertes and Polonius, Hamlet has his first words: '*A little more than kin, and less than kind.*' While all the cast up until that point had spoken their lines in a loud, almost declamatory, manner, Jared Root mumbled his, as though he were in a television rehearsal.

No one said anything about his delivery, but it put the other actors off their stride. For them to continue in their full-throttled way looked as if it were showing up their star. So they started to rein back their performances to match his. By the time they reached the stage direction for the end of the scene – *Exeunt all except Hamlet* – Claudius and Gertrude were also mumbling. And the entire company were waiting with bated breath to see how Jared Root would tackle the first great soliloquy, '*O! that this too too solid flesh would melt . . .*'

To their surprise, when they got to the cue the winner of *Top Pop* announced, 'I'm not going to do this now.'

'What!' said a flabbergasted Ned English. Then to Milly Henryson, 'Stop the watch. Why are you not going to read the soliloquy, Jared? We need you to, to get an overall timing.'

'I haven't worked on it yet,' said the singer.

'I know you haven't,' responded the director. 'No one else has worked on their lines yet. This is the first day of rehearsal.'

'Yeah, but I don't want to do the long bits till I've worked on them with my coach.'

'Coach?' echoed Ned.

'My acting coach.'

'You have an acting coach?'

'Of course. And I need to work with him on the long bits.'

'But, Jared, I am directing this production.'

'Sure.'

'So I will be telling you how to say the lines, not some acting coach.'

'But I've been working with him since I won *Top Pop*.'

'I don't care whether you've been working with him since

you were in nappies!' Ned English was by now looking very angry. 'This is a read-through for my production of *Hamlet*. I need the entire script to be read out loud – including the soliloquies.'

'Is that what the long bits are called?'

'Yes, Jared, it is.'

'Well, I'm not going to read them. Not till I've done some work on them with my coach.'

'I think you will find, Jared,' stormed the director, 'that, according to your contract, you are obliged to—'

'Don't worry,' interposed a conciliatory voice. 'If Jared doesn't want to read the soliloquies now, let someone else read them, just for your timing.'

Ned English began to remonstrate, but he only got as far as: 'But—' Then, since the speaker had been Tony Copeland, he instantly kowtowed and said, 'Very well. Start the watch again.'

He then proceeded to read Hamlet's first soliloquy as though it were a telephone directory or a shopping list.

Charles Paris exchanged looks with other members of the cast and knew that they were all thinking the same thing. The scene they had just witnessed between the director and the singer had been a power struggle. And if Jared Root had Tony Copeland on his side, then there was no doubt who would really be calling the shots.

The read-through continued rather dismally. Inhibited, the actors held back from giving full-bodied performances. Charles did not feel he could let rip as the Ghost. And each time they came to another of the soliloquies Jared Root sat back and let Ned English struggle through the lines.

But in spite of the circumstances Charles Paris still revelled in the richness of Shakespeare's language and began to feel optimistic that the play would somehow win through. Maybe Jared Root's 'acting coach' would turn out to be very good at his job and coax a decent performance out of the young man. Or maybe the scene they'd just witnessed had been no more than Jared asserting his power. Having done that, he might knuckle down and work properly with Ned on his interpretation of Hamlet.

Charles was also looking forward to the Gravediggers' scene. After considerable deliberation, he had decided to go for the voice he'd used as the Head Gardener in some dire stage thriller ('Charles Paris's accent was as creaky as the plot.' – *Blackpool Citizen*), and he was hoping to get the odd laugh during the reading.

But before they reached his moment there was another hiccup in the proceedings. They had just read Act IV Scene iv and were about to read Ophelia's Mad Scene when Katrina Selsey said, 'Oh, I had a thought about this.'

'Stop the watch!' said the director. But he didn't sound too testy. Katrina's vowels might need a little ironing-out before she could pass as a member of the Danish court, but the reading so far had shown her to be a good little actress (oops – actor). *StarHunt*'s selection process had been vindicated and with a bit of work she could become a moving – and even memorable – Ophelia.

So it was benignly that Ned asked, 'What is it, Katrina?'

'Well, it's these songs she sings.'

'Yes, well, they are traditional ditties of the time. But the original tunes have been lost, so . . .' he announced, as if presenting her with a rich gift, 'I'm having new tunes specially composed for them.'

'But the thing is . . .' said Katrina.

'Yes . . .?'

'She's, like, round the twist, isn't she?'

'I'm not sure that I'd put it like that, but she's certainly suffering from some form of mental illness, yes.'

'So what she sings is, like, gibberish, isn't it?'

'Well, not exactly.'

'The words don't mean anything.'

'No, Katrina, they do have thematic relevance to other ideas in the play and—'

'But what I'm saying is that she doesn't really know what she's singing . . .'

'Perhaps not,' Ned English conceded cautiously.

'. . . so she could be singing anything.'

'We-ell . . .'

'So I suggested to Peri – and she thought it was a really

great idea – that rather than singing the songs we've got here, I should sing some of the ones from my forthcoming album.'

The rehearsal room lapsed into a stunned silence.

'I have got a record deal,' Katrina insisted.

'So have I,' Jared Root riposted waspishly. 'And my sales are already bigger than yours are ever likely to be. Pre-orders for my new album are going stratospheric.'

'I've got thousands of followers on Twitter,' said Katrina with defiance.

'Thousands?' Jared Root echoed witheringly. 'I've got millions.'

Charles Paris caught the eye of Geraldine Romelle opposite and was rewarded by a mischievous smile. If they'd ever doubted it, they both now knew for certain that rehearsals for Tony Copeland Productions' *Hamlet* were going to be a long, arduous process.

FIVE

'Frances, it's Charles.'

    'Hello, stranger.'

    'And what is that meant to mean?'

'It's meant to mean it has been a while since you've rung me.'

'Really? A few weeks, maybe.'

'Make that months.'

'Oh.'

'Four months, nearer five, actually.'

'Oh.'

'Anyway, to what do I owe this sudden honour?'

'Well, I have been rehearsing.'

'Is that an excuse, Charles?'

'It's more of a fact.'

'And a way of telling me that you have actually got some work for once?'

    'I suppose it is that too, yes.'

    'So what is it you're doing?'

Charles gave his wife the edited highlights of *Hamlet*'s journey to the Grand Theatre, Marlborough, where the play was due to open in a couple of days' time. It was Monday and he was in the middle of an interminable Technical Rehearsal (universally referred to in the theatre as the 'Tech'). The interior-of-a-cranium set, which had looked so splendid in the model, was proving difficult to fit into a real theatre – or at least to fit in such a way that all the required lighting effects could be achieved. And the designer, who saw all the problems as being caused by the local Marlborough stage crew not matching up to West End standards, was not helping to achieve an easy working atmosphere. Ned English was tearing his hair out at the Tech's lengthening delays.

    'Well, at least,' said Frances at the end of Charles's narrative, 'it's going to mean another straight play in the West End, which has to be good news. Not another jukebox musical or cobbled-together evening featuring the winners of some television talent show.'

'Except it is that in a way.' And Charles told her how Katrina Selsey had come to be playing Ophelia.

'Ah,' said Frances. 'I haven't seen it, but I've heard of that show, *StarHunt*. A lot of my pupils seem to be hooked on it. Which I suppose is a good thing because at least it means they get to hear some Shakespeare. But it doesn't sound to me like a good way of casting something like *Hamlet*. I mean, I can see it might work for a musical, but for a straight play . . .'

'I'm right with you on that.'

'So how is your Ophelia?'

'She's actually not bad, you know, as an actor.'

'Oh, for heaven's sake, Charles. I never thought I'd hear you referring to an "actress" as an "actor".'

'You have to be very careful in my profession now, Frances. It's absolutely crawling with feminists.'

'Not before time.'

'Maybe not.'

'And what about your Hamlet?'

'What about him?'

'I read somewhere in the press that he also came up through some television talent show.'

'Yes, he did.'

'In fact, I seem to have read quite a lot about him in the press. Him and the Ophelia.'

'Yes, there has been quite a bit.'

It was true, Charles reflected. He'd been in many productions, quite a few involving big stars, but he'd never witnessed a pre-publicity blitz on the scale that this *Hamlet* was receiving. Not that the press were interested in anything about the play except for the fact that Jared Root and – to a lesser extent – Katrina Selsey were in it. And their coverage tended to mention *StarHunt* and *Top Pop* and Jared's forthcoming album more than they did *Hamlet*. But television talent shows clearly did nurture interest in a demographic which didn't normally go to the theatre. And, although Charles Paris didn't fully understand what Facebook and Twitter were, he gathered there was a lot of activity there too.

Still, he shouldn't complain. The show's high profile had had a stimulating effect at the box office. The four-week tour was virtually sold out, and the advance in the West End was much higher than for the average straight play.

As presaged at the read-through, there had been more conflict between Hamlet and Ophelia as to which of them was getting the most publicity. Jared Root was winning – he had after all been in the public eye for a year longer than Katrina and his first album was already out – but he was clearly anxious about his rival's growing popularity. The envy between the two of them had not made for a relaxed atmosphere during rehearsals.

'But what I want to know about your Hamlet,' said Frances, 'is: is he any good?'

There was a long silence. Then Charles said, 'Pass.'

'Right. *Hamlet* without the Prince, is it?'

'I think it'd be rather better if it were *Hamlet* without the Prince.'

'That bad, huh?'

'Not great.' Charles thought back to the agonies of the previous four weeks' rehearsal. 'Maybe his performance will come up when he's playing the show with an audience,' he tried to convince himself. Then, changing the subject, he said, 'Anyway, I was thinking it might be nice for us to meet up.'

'Why, Charles?'

'Well, because we're married, apart from anything else.'

Bad argument, he realized as Frances responded, 'For some couples that would certainly be a reason for meeting. I'm not sure that it works with us.'

'How can you say that? We do have a bit of history, don't we?'

'Most married couples have a bit of history.'

'Well, then . . .'

'But with many of them that history is of moments shared, things done together – not a long sequence of separations, failed rapprochements and further separations.'

'Is that how you see our marriage, Frances?'

'Is there another way of seeing it?'

'Well, you know, I've always thought, yes, we may have had our ups and downs, but still there's—'

'Don't be fatuous, Charles.'

'Oh, was I being fatuous?'

'Yes.'

'Ah. Well, I thought there was still quite a lot of love there.'

'Not the kind of love that sustains relationships.'

'And what kind is that?'

'I think you're being deliberately naive, Charles. The love I'm talking about involves proximity, for a start. "Being there" – have you heard the expression?'

'Well, yes, but the nature of an actor's work inevitably involves long periods of absence.'

'And for how much of the last five months has your work as an actor involved your being away from London?'

'Um. We've been rehearsing in Marlborough for the last two days.'

'Really?'

'And I did do a day's filming at Newlands Corner a few weeks back.'

'Hm. That seems to leave quite a bit of the last five months unaccounted for.'

'I can see you could see it that way,' Charles conceded.

'So who was she?'

'Who was who?'

'Come on, Charles. In the past when there've been long silences from you, it's frequently because there's been some woman involved. It's only when she finally sees the light and chucks you that you come crawling back to me.'

'Now that's not fair, Frances.'

'Do you want me to give you names?'

'No, no,' he replied hastily. 'Anyway, I can assure you there hasn't been anything of that kind for ages. Worse luck.'

He knew he shouldn't have added those last two words, and the broadside he received from his wife made absolutely clear to him why he shouldn't have added them. When she had finally calmed down enough for him to get a word in, he said, 'I promise there aren't any other women currently on my horizon.'

To be completely truthful, his sentence would have depended a bit on how you defined the word 'horizon'. Charles Paris was still finding Geraldine Romelle very attractive, and the occasional shared smile or giggle during rehearsals had suggested that she was not completely immune to his charms. But at the end of every day in the Kilburn barracks, she never joined him and some of the others for a drink. She always seemed to have somewhere to go back to. Whether that also meant she had someone to go back to, Charles didn't know. She didn't wear a wedding ring . . . not that that meant anything. But her availability was something he intended to investigate once the show was up and running in Marlborough. Even if Geraldine Romelle did have someone in London, DCOL also applied to touring. DCOT perhaps it should be. 'Doesn't Count On Tour.'

Charles became aware of a long silence from the other end of the phone. Then Frances asked, 'So what are you suggesting?'

'Well, as I said, I just thought it'd be nice for us to meet.'

'When? You're now in Marlborough and you've just told me you're going to be out on tour for the next five weeks.'

'Yes, but then we come into the West End.'

'So?'

'Well, the West End is in London.'

'Thank you, Charles. I'd never have worked that out for myself.'

'Ha, ha. But I was thinking maybe we could meet up then . . .?'

'Hm. Let me think about that for a moment.' She thought about it for a moment. 'Do you remember last time you suggested we meet up?'

'No, I can't say I do.'

'We had a conversation similar to the one we've just had.'

'Did we?'

'Yes, very similar. And eventually I agreed to meet you and you said you'd call me the next day with what you called the "fine tuning", when and where, that kind of thing.'

'And when was this?'

'Five months ago.'

Charles Paris didn't actually think the conversation had gone very well.

*   *   *

The Grand Theatre, Marlborough, built in Victorian times, had played host to a huge variety of entertainments over the years. Like most regional theatres it had gone through many cycles of closure and dilapidation, followed by refurbishment and new hope. The finances of such a building were always going to be precarious, but its latest renewal had been courtesy of substantial grants from the local council. (The Arts Council had been approached, but helping a regional theatre had not been part of their mission statement at the time. It was their refusal to provide funding which had brought to the local authorities a wake-up call and a realization that they might be about to lose an important part of Marlborough's heritage. That had spurred them into action.) The improved facilities had led to the Grand becoming a regular staging post on the Tony Copeland Productions touring circuit, so at least its short-term future looked set fair.

Charles Paris loved old theatres. Though he'd never admit it to anyone, he got quite sentimental about them. The newer concrete cathedrals of the drama might be better designed, even have better acoustics, but for Charles they could never match the cavernous mustiness of an old building like the Grand. He loved fantasizing about the productions staged there: the triumphs, the tragedies, the reputations made and ruined, the love fallen into, the hearts broken. But his customary shell of cynicism rarely allowed him to share such thoughts.

'I'm sorry, Jared, but you still can't be heard from the back of the auditorium.' Ned English's voice was very weary. From the first day of rehearsal at the Kilburn barracks he had been on at his Hamlet about audibility. Or at least he'd been on at him in a very gentle way. The director had been rendered cautious by the scene at the run-through when it had become so clear that Jared Root had Tony Copeland firmly in his corner. Ned was very keen not to upset his star or his star's protector, but he was also very keen to stop him from mumbling.

They were in the Green Room, during another of the longueurs while a section of the cranium set had to be adjusted to allow it to be properly lit. As Charles Paris had prognosticated, though the set perfectly matched the structure of a human skull, nature's design had not been intended to fit into a theatre – at least not into the Grand Theatre, Marlborough. The frontal bone, the two parietal bones, the two temporal bones and occipital bone which joined up so neatly in the model proved to be less accommodating in their giant reality. And when they did fit together, they were proving very difficult to light.

Clearly, all was not going well on stage. The Green Room tannoy speaker was turned down low, but there was still a background noise of rumbles, clanks, arguments and muttered expletives. An intermittent three-way row was going on between the designer, the lighting designer and a tall lugubrious shaggy-haired stagehand called Bazza, who seemed to be in charge of fitting the skull set on to the stage of the Grand Theatre. The language flying back and forth was distinctly industrial.

Charles Paris, inured over the years to the tedium of Techs and mellowed by the couple of illicit pints he had snuck out for during the lunch-break, was trying in a desultory fashion to do *The Times* crossword and finding that his eyes kept gliding over the clues.

A few seats along from him, Dennis Demetriades was avidly pressing the buttons of his mobile. Charles was constantly amazed by how much time the younger generation of actors could spend texting or whatever else it was they were doing with their phones. He never saw any of them with a book or a newspaper. Dennis, Charles noticed, had changed his facial topiary. The thick black stubble had been allowed to grow to the contours but not the density of mutton chop whiskers. Their forward points joined a thin line of moustache across his upper lips. The young actor, Charles reckoned, must have to get up very early to tend his beard garden.

On the other side of the Green Room sat Geraldine Romelle, immersed in a copy of Montaigne's *Essays*. Her choice of reading matter rather intrigued Charles. Was she a genuine intellectual or one of those actresses all of whose ideas came from other people and who would uncomprehendingly read a difficult book 'because this really great guy recommended it to me'?

As the argument between Ned English and his Hamlet continued, Charles and Geraldine were both doing something that actors are quite skilled at – taking in every word of a conversation without apparently listening.

'I'd be heard perfectly from the back of the auditorium,' said Jared Root, 'if you have me miked.'

Dennis Demetriades wasn't distracted from his mobile, but the two other actors exchanged surreptitious looks. Charles and Geraldine were both old enough to know about the value of 'projection' in the theatre, and both quite capable (particularly in their cups) of going on at length about the new generation of actors who spent so much time working for television that their voices 'just aren't trained to fill a theatre'. The covert looks the two exchanged became covert smiles as they waited for Ned English's response.

'Jared,' he said, 'may I remind you once again that we're putting on a straight play here, not a musical? And not any straight play either, but one of the greatest plays in the English – or indeed any other – language. The part of Hamlet has been acted by generations of the most famous actors in the world – and none of them needed electronic aids to ensure that they were heard at the back of the auditorium.'

'But that's an old style of acting,' argued Jared Root. 'Belting the words out. It's corny and unnatural. I've been tweeting about it and my followers aren't going to want to see something they can't hear.'

'No, but, Jared, if you projected properly they would be able to hear. It's really not difficult. I'm sure if you made an effort—'

'Listen, Ned,' said the singer in a tone that implied he was being entirely reasonable, 'audiences – particularly young audiences – are used to watching television where people act more like they're just talking than, you know, like, declaiming.'

'That may be true, Jared, but the theatre audience is used to a different experience. They—'

'That's what the *old* theatre audience are used to, right.

But if you want an audience that isn't just made up of old farts – and that's what Tony has said quite definitely he wants with this production – then you've got to present younger people with something that they're, like, used to seeing. And they're used to seeing people acting naturally, and the only way you're going to achieve that in a great big theatre like this is by using mikes.'

'Jared,' said an exasperated Ned English, 'for the last time, there will be no mikes in this production of *Hamlet*.'

'Huh,' the star responded. 'I'll see what Tony Copeland thinks about that.'

With which parting shot, Jared Root left the Green Room. Still texting away, Dennis Demetriades also shuffled out. With an apologetic smile to no one in particular, Ned English bustled off after them. If Jared was appealing to the show's producer, the director could envisage a lot more problems ahead.

While Ned had remained in the room, Charles Paris and Geraldine Romelle had been studiously studying, respectively, *The Times* crossword and Montaigne's *Essays*. But the minute he was out of the door they exchanged looks and both collapsed into hysterical giggles.

'Well,' said Charles when he had recovered the ability to speak, 'what next? And what the hell does "tweeting" mean?'

Geraldine Romelle grinned. 'I'll explain it to you when you're older, Charles.'

'Thanks very much. I must say, a conversation like the one we've just heard makes me feel as if I'm well past my sell-by date. Shakespeare with mikes? Why should we stop at that? Why not turn *Hamlet* into a full-scale musical?'

'It has been done,' said Geraldine.

'Has it?'

'Well, no, not really. But there was a version written by John Poole in 1810 called *Hamlet Travestie*, in which "To be or not to be" was set to music.'

'Really?' said Charles, quickly deciding that Geraldine Romelle was a genuine intellectual rather than just a voguish actress.

'Yes. It begins:

"When a man becomes tir'd of his life,
The question is 'to be or not to be?'
For before he dare finish the strife,
His reflections most serious ought to be.
When his troubles too numerous grow,
And he knows of no method to mend them,
Had he best bear them tamely or no
Or by stoutly opposing them end them?"

'Then it goes into a chorus beginning, *"Ri tol de rol . . ."* and so on through a great many other verses.'

'How on earth do you know that?'

'Oh, I did a dissertation on parody versions of *Hamlet* when I was at Cambridge.'

'Really?' Charles Paris was becoming even more interested in Geraldine Romelle with every word she spoke. 'I'd love to hear more about that.'

'I'm sure that would be possible.'

'Maybe . . .' he began casually, 'we could meet up for a drink once we get to the end of this wretched Tech . . .?'

The expression on Geraldine Romelle's face suggested that she was about to agree to his suggestion, which in Charles's view would be a great step forward. But before Geraldine could shape the words of her response, from the tannoy speaker came the sound of an enormous crash followed by confused shouting.

'What the hell's that?' asked Geraldine Romelle.

'Something on stage,' replied Charles as he led the way out of the Green Room.

When he reached the backstage area the shouting had stopped, to be replaced by a shocked silence.

Part of the set, one of the giant skull's parietal bones, a concave structure of wood and fibreglass, had crashed down from the flies.

On the wooden boards of the stage, poking out from underneath it, were the legs of Jared Root. They showed no signs of movement.

SIX

It was fortunate that the designer of *Hamlet* had modelled his set so closely on the human cranium. But for the concavity of the skull segment that landed on him, Jared Root would have been much more severely injured. A flat section of the same weight falling from the same height would undoubtedly have killed him. As it was, the wood-reinforced edge of fibreglass shell caught him a glancing blow on the shoulder. Though the impact of this broke his collar bone and fractured his right tibia, the hollowness of the structure meant that he suffered no head injuries.

There was no doubt, however, that Jared would not be able to continue with the show. Early estimations of his recovery time were in months rather than weeks. Tony Copeland's production was now in the situation Frances had suggested – '*Hamlet* without the Prince'.

But, remarkably, the Tech of the show continued. Ned English – acting, Charles Paris presumed, on instructions from Tony in London – passed on the news to the company, who had been called into the Green Room once Jared Root was on his way to the hospital.

'But how can we do it without Jared?' objected Katrina Selsey. '*Hamlet* is in, like, quite a few of the scenes.'

'Will can stand in.'

Charles looked across at the ASM. Oh yes, of course, as well as being Second Gravedigger, he was officially Jared Root's understudy. And from the expression on the young man's face, Will Portlock's most treasured fantasy had just become reality. In the boy's mind the *A Star Is Born* scenario was being acted out, newspaper headlines were writing themselves. 'Unknown steps in and triumphs!' Jared Root's misfortune would provide the basis for Will Portlock's fortune.

The visions in Charles Paris's mind were less rosy. He'd witnessed too many shows where the official understudy had thought he'd got the job, only for the producer to ace him out at the last minute and replace him with a bigger name. It had happened more than once to Charles himself. He remembered particularly the bitterness he'd felt after giving an excellent performance in a play called *The Hooded Owl* at the Prince's Theatre Taunton, only to be demoted to understudy by a better-known actor when the play transferred to the West End.

And even if the understudy did get the part, triumph was not the inevitable outcome. The review Charles'd got when replacing a senior actor sidelined with appendicitis in one of Shakespeare's Roman Plays still rankled. 'With Charles Paris as Julius Caesar, I was surprised Brutus and his cronies didn't take action earlier.' – *Beeston Express*.

So the Tech continued on its customary route of frustration. Actors are very good at shrinking into a kind of zombie state during Techs. Most of them understand that at that stage of a production, the focus is not on them. They may be required to stand around on stage for a long time while lighting effects are tested, and to repeat the same lines endlessly while the timings of set changes and sound cues are refined. The process is boring and it can take a very long time, but experienced actors know it's just part of the job. At such times very few of them even attempt to give a full-power performance. They hold that in reserve for the Dress Rehearsal and subsequent exposure to an audience.

Which was why Charles Paris found it interesting to see how Will Portlock behaved during the Tech. The young actor was giving his Hamlet full-on. What was more, he knew the words – which wasn't always the case with understudies at that stage of a production. Understudy rehearsals are meant to take place during the main rehearsal period, but frequently, given the pressure of getting the show itself on with the regular cast, they get overlooked. And, because he was understudying Polonius, Charles knew for a fact that no understudy rehearsals had yet taken place for the Tony Copeland Productions' *Hamlet*.

But Will Portlock had clearly taken his job seriously. He knew every move that Jared Root had rehearsed. And, rather than just walking through a Tech, he acted the part of Hamlet as if he were auditioning for it. Which, Charles reflected, perhaps he was. After all, until countermanding orders were received from Tony Copeland in London, Will Portlock was playing the part.

Charles hoped the boy wasn't in for a big disappointment.

He found himself standing in the wings next to Will during a long hiatus while the interior cranium lighting was adjusted for the scene in Gertrude's closet.

'Well done,' he said. 'You're giving it lots of welly.'

'Wouldn't you if you were given the chance to play Hamlet?'

'Not sure I would for a Tech.'

'Look, Charles, in two days I'm going to be playing the part to a paying audience. I need to be full on for all the rehearsal time I can get.'

'You may be right.'

'Have you ever actually played the part?'

A wry shake of the head. Hamlet wasn't the kind of part actors like Charles Paris got. Even when he was the right age for it, the nearest he'd come was Horatio. ('Charles Paris played Horatio like a particularly slow-witted Dr Watson.' – *Oldham Evening Chronicle*.)

'Well, this is a big opportunity for me,' said Will Portlock earnestly, 'and I'm not going to waste it.'

'Good for you.'

'I've texted my father about it. He's flying over from Baltimore for the First Night on Wednesday.'

Charles just hoped that the insurance covered last-minute cancellation of the flight if that became necessary.

'I'm very determined to make a success of my career,' were Will Portlock's last words before rehearsal of the Closet Scene was allowed to resume.

The intensity with which they were said brought a new thought into Charles's head. Will's preparedness to take over as Hamlet suggested an unusual degree of forethought. And what had happened to the originally cast Hamlet had been nothing but good news for his young understudy. For the first time Charles Paris found himself idly wondering just how accidental Jared Root's injuries had been.

SEVEN

C harles had been unprepared for the level of publicity attracted by the accident at the Grand Theatre, Marlborough. There was a camera crew at the Stage Door within an hour of Jared Root's departure in the ambulance, and apparently another one at the hospital to which he had been taken. News of his injuries made radio and television news bulletins. And apparently Facebook and Twitter were alive with reactions to the subject.

This last information Charles did not find out for himself, but heard from younger members of the company. It wasn't just Jared and Katrina who counted their followers on Twitter. It seemed that having a presence on social media was essential for every actor under a certain age. And a good few over that age. Charles Paris had been surprised to discover in conversation with Geraldine Romelle that she was on Facebook and Twitter. 'Have to keep in the loop, darling,' she had said to him when the subject came up.

He was slightly annoyed that the commotion following Jared Root's injury had prevented him and Geraldine having their promised drink together. He hoped the occasion was simply postponed, but she didn't mention it during the rest of the delayed Tech. And Charles was beginning to feel an increasing need for feminine companionship. Or actually, to call a spade a spade, sex.

He looked around for Geraldine when the Tech did finally end, but there was no sign of her. Granted, it was by then nearly two in the morning, so the thought of adjourning to some local hostelry was out of the question. But, cynical and embittered though he was, Charles Paris sometimes entertained fantasies about women as unrealistic as those he did about his career. The idea that Geraldine Romelle might have invited him back to her digs for 'a nightcap' was, of course, ridiculous, but he was childishly disappointed that she'd left the theatre without saying goodnight to him. He felt alone and maudlin, depressed by the knowledge that he would now inevitably go back to his digs and drink too much from the bottle of Bell's that awaited him there.

Before leaving the theatre he went to the Green Room in the last despairing hope that he might find Geraldine. Of course, he didn't, but sitting in there was the pretty young ASM, Milly Henryson. Like everyone else of her age who had a spare moment, she was fiddling about with her mobile phone.

She looked up from the screen at his entrance and grinned. 'Hi, Charles.'

The thought of inviting her for a drink somewhere was instinctive but, by good fortune, quickly rejected. Milly Henryson really was too young for him, and Charles was getting to the age where unwanted advances could all too easily look like the actions of a dirty old man.

He was again struck by the ease with which she talked to him, which he'd felt from the read-through onwards. He was again sure that they must have met before that, but again totally unable to remember where. Oh dear, that kind of thing was happening increasingly as he got older.

'I was just checking Twitter,' the girl said. 'Lots more reactions to what happened to Jared.'

'Ah.' Charles hoped the monosyllable conveyed to her his complete familiarity with what on earth she was talking about.

'There's even one from him,' Milly went on.

'How could he do that?'

'He'll have his mobile with him.'

'Yes, but I'd have thought, given how badly injured he is . . .'

The girl shrugged. 'Well, it's definitely from him. It's got his Twitter handle.'

Charles Paris let out another 'Ah' which he hoped would give the same knowledgeable impression as the first one. 'What does he say?'

'Just thanks for all the messages of goodwill he's had from his followers.'

Followers? thought Charles. Who the hell does Jared Root think he is? The bloody Messiah?

'Hm,' Milly went on, 'he doesn't mention *Hamlet*.'

'So?'

'Well, it could be good publicity for the show.'

'His accident you mean?'

'Yes, it could really give the box office a boost,' said the girl, unaware that she was sounding a little bit callous. 'But,' she concluded in a disappointed tone, 'in this tweet he only mentions *Top Pop*. And his new album.'

'Ah,' said Charles Paris.

He left the Grand Theatre without making anything that could be even vaguely interpreted as an expression of sexual interest in Milly Henryson. And that made him feel perversely virtuous.

Charles woke in his digs to a text message from the Stage Manager, saying that there would be a full company call onstage at eleven a.m. This was no surprise as everyone wanted to know the future direction of the *Hamlet* production as soon as possible. Would Will Portlock keep his recently won role? Or was Tony Copeland about to parachute in another big name from London? Would the Marlborough performances start in two days' time as per schedule, or would the opening be postponed?

Predictably enough, Charles Paris had woken with a hangover. Not one of the big agonizing brain-crushers, just a local pain on the inside of his cranium, possibly adjacent to one of the parietal bones. He wasn't so immobilized that he couldn't face a black Americano and bacon roll picked up at a café on his way to the theatre, but it was still mildly annoying. Stupid to have been drinking so late at night. And on his own. He wondered what it would feel like to wake up without any kind of hangover. There's a novelty, he thought. When had that last happened to him? He couldn't remember.

There was a considerable buzz of anticipation and, in some cases, anxiety round the auditorium of the Grand Theatre, where the *Hamlet* company had been instructed to sit. Like Charles, a lot of the other actors held cardboard coffee cups. Those who didn't held that other young actor's essential, a bottle of water. Many of them were, of course, texting manically on mobile phones.

Charles looked round the assembled throng. He caught the

eye of Geraldine Romelle, who smiled at him. An automatic smile, though, nothing special about it. Katrina Selsey was looking very pleased with herself, positively glowing with confidence. Maybe to her mind, Charles conjectured, the removal of Jared Root from the scene had left her as the only 'celebrity' in the cast . . .?

Will Portlock's expression was one of understandable nervousness. Given the time pressure, his future either as Hamlet or reverting to his humble position of Second Gravedigger and ASM must be decided soon. And his father's flight from Baltimore either confirmed or cancelled. His tense expression suggested that he had been given no prior warning of what decision had been taken.

Near Will sat Milly Henryson, her dark-blue eyes glowing with excitement. Charles wondered what had happened overnight to bring her that sparkle. His first thought was sex. Yes, someone as beautiful as Milly must have a boyfriend. Lucky bugger. Charles felt infinitely old. And he also again felt sure he'd met the girl before the *Hamlet* read-through.

The company was not kept in suspense for long. On the dot of eleven o'clock, Ned English came onstage from the wings, ushering in Tony Copeland and Doug Haye, the silent man from Tony Copeland Productions who'd been at the read-through. Accompanying them, and taking the fourth chair set on the stage, was a young man whom Charles recognized. He had blond hair and pale eyelashes, very Nordic-looking.

'Good morning, everyone,' said Ned. Then, recognizing his own humble and subsidiary role in the proceedings, he handed straight over to the show's producer.

'Good morning,' said Tony Copeland. 'I've just come from the hospital where I've been visiting Jared. He had surgery last night, so he's still in a fairly woozy state, but he did ask me to thank all of you who sent him goodwill messages. I spoke to his doctor and fortunately there seems a very good prospect that Jared will make a complete recovery.'

Charles couldn't see who started it, but this news was greeted by an apparently spontaneous round of applause from the auditorium.

'But, of course,' the producer continued, 'that recovery is

not going to happen overnight. We're talking in terms of months rather than weeks, which obviously means there's no way Jared's going to be our Hamlet in this production.'

There was a silence, and Charles Paris was aware of the tension in the young man sitting next to Tony Copeland.

'So we need a new Hamlet – and at this kind of notice we need someone who knows all the lines, in fact someone who has played the part recently. And I'm glad I've been able to find just such a person.' The producer gestured to the young man at his side. 'You won't know his name yet, but let me tell you the world of the theatre soon will. I don't often make predictions about future success, but I saw the production of *Hamlet* in which this gentleman played the Prince – and I saw star quality. So may I introduce to you the actor who will be taking over the part of Hamlet in this production with immediate effect – Sam Newton-Reid!'

Charles's first reaction was one of gratified relief. So it was still possible for genuine talent to make its way through the clutter of celebrity hype and be rewarded. He remembered the young actor in the Battersea pub saying he'd hoped Tony Copeland might come and see his Hamlet. That's what must have happened. Charles's respect for the producer increased.

He also remembered then where it was that he had first met Milly Henryson – she was Sam Newton-Reid's girlfriend; she had been playing Ophelia in the Battersea pub *Hamlet* – and he understood the suffused excitement he'd noticed in her that morning.

But his strongest impression in the aftermath of Tony Copeland's announcement was the look of blind fury on the face of Will Portlock, who had just had perhaps the greatest part in the whole Shakespearean canon snatched away from him. And the larceny had happened in public, without anything in the way of prior warning or apology. Will's father would have to cancel his flight from Baltimore.

'Oh, for God's sake, Charles. Do you just not notice other people?'

'Yes, of course I notice them, but seeing them out of context . . .'

'It's only five months ago that you spent an hour in a bar in Battersea with Milly after watching her boyfriend's Hamlet.'

'I knew I'd seen her somewhere. I just forgot.'

'There seem to be quite a lot of things you forget in the evenings, Charles.'

'Oh, and what's that meant to mean?'

'It's meant to mean that during our occasional periods of cohabitation—'

'Now that's not fair. We lived together for a lot of—'

'During our occasional periods of cohabitation, Charles, I remember many times when I told you things in the evening of which you claimed to have no recollection the following morning.'

'And what do you put that down to?'

'Far be it from me to say.'

'Are you suggesting that the booze . . .?'

'I didn't say it, Charles. You did.'

He wondered whether she had a point. There had been times when his recollection of evening conversations had been a bit hazy the day after. Yes, he thought righteously, I must cut down on the booze. And get back with Frances on a more permanent basis. How often had he said that?

'Anyway, Frances, I'm intrigued how you already know about Sam taking over. There hasn't been time for the press to get hold of the story yet.'

'Milly tweeted about it.'

'"Tweeted"? Is that to do with Twitter?' asked Charles.

'Well done. Are you telling me that you're finally coming into the twenty-first century, Charles?'

He was aghast. 'Frances, are you implying that you – my wife – use Twitter?'

'Of course. Remember, I'm headmistress of a girls' school. How else am I going to find out what my pupils are up to?' Charles was still too shocked to respond as she went on, 'I hadn't heard from Milly for a while, otherwise I would have known that she was working in the same production as you, but she couldn't resist telling me about Sam taking over as Hamlet.'

'Right.'

There was a silence. 'Anyway, how are you getting on with your Gertrude?'

'What do you mean?'

'Charles, I know *Hamlet*. The only cast member round your age has got to be Gertrude. So unless you're doing more cradle-snatching, Gertrude must be the one you're interested in.'

Her logic was uncomfortably close to the truth. 'Oh, for heaven's sake,' he blustered, 'don't imagine that I try to get off with women in every production I'm involved in. What do you take me for?'

'Do you really want me to answer that, Charles?'

'Well, no, I . . .' He converted his confusion into laughter, as if what she'd said was a very good joke. 'Anyway,' he continued joshingly, 'why would I need to be interested in other women when I've got you?'

'And to what extent do you think you've "got" me, Charles?'

Another question that didn't invite an easy answer. Imbuing his voice with maximum sincerity, he said, 'I really think we should meet.'

As she had during their previous phone conversation, Frances asked, 'Why?'

EIGHT

Ned English's rehearsal plan for the Tuesday afternoon was to walk through the whole play, integrating Sam Newton-Reid into the action. Though the young actor knew the lines, his previous Hamlet had been performed in the small upstairs room of a pub, not on the stage of the Grand Theatre, Marlborough inside his own cranium. He needed to learn the moves that Jared Root and the rest of the cast had been rehearsing for some weeks.

That work would stop in time for the actors to have their Equity-required break before the evening's scheduled Dress Rehearsal. But, accommodating a new Hamlet, that Dress Rehearsal was bound to be a much interrupted affair. With such minimal preparation, there was no way the play could open the next day, as scheduled. So the Wednesday evening would witness a hopefully less disjointed Dress Rehearsal, and the First Night in front of the paying public would be postponed till the Thursday. Given the publicity surrounding Jared Root's accident, no one in the general public would be much surprised by the change of plan.

The new production timetable was communicated to the company by the stage management, who said that Ned English had made the decision to postpone – though Charles was of the view that the director was just passing on the orders he'd been given by Tony Copeland. Even with the extra day, it remained a tight schedule, particularly for the new Hamlet, Sam Newton-Reid.

The company were called to start work at two o'clock on the Tuesday afternoon, so after Tony Copeland's pep talk, Charles Paris reckoned he had time for a couple of pints for the necessary irrigation of his brain. He had worked in Marlborough before and remembered a small pub not far from the theatre where he had filled many an idle hour on his previous visit. He hoped it was still open. So many pubs had given up the unequal struggle and closed during the past few years.

As he snuck out of the Grand Theatre's Stage Door, Charles realized it was the first time on this visit that a break in rehearsals had given him the chance to go out into Marlborough, and he was reminded what a pretty place it was. The archetypal English market town, its very wide High Street was flanked by tall, mostly Georgian buildings in mellow red brick, with the Town Hall at one end and Marlborough College at the other. The school was so much part of the town that there always seemed to be lots of pupils milling about the place. Except on market days, the central strip of the High Street was filled with parked cars.

But it wasn't one of the posh tarted-up tourist pubs on the main drag that Charles Paris was looking for. Relying on a distant memory, he set off into the back streets down towards the River Kennet.

To his relief he found the pub was still there, looking as unprepossessing as ever it had. Charles was pleased about that. He hadn't welcomed the gentrification and gastrification which had been the fate of so many pubs (like those on Marlborough High Street). Charles Paris took the old-fashioned view that fine dining should be done in restaurants and that pubs should stick to their traditional role of supplying alcohol and tasteless bar snacks. Sometimes, when he was with people, he enjoyed a bit of atmosphere in his drinking hole. On his own, the drabber the venue the better. When he drank alone, he needed shabby surroundings to match his mood. He recalled that during his previous stint at the Grand Theatre Marlborough he'd nicknamed the pub The Pessimist's Arms.

From recollection of that time Charles might have expected to see other members of the company in the bar when he entered. But his earlier visit to Marlborough had been a long while ago and times had changed. Now almost no actors would go out for a lunchtime drink on a working day. A distressing number of them didn't even have any alcohol when unwinding at the *end* of a working day. They just all walked round with their eternal bottles of water. And spent any spare time they had in the gym. Unless you were bulking up for some part that involved taking your shirt off, Charles couldn't understand what business it was of an actor ever to step inside a gym.

Fortunately, the pub was almost exactly as he remembered it. A surly, unsmiling barman and a lot of men drinking on their own, uninterested in anyone else in the bar. An unwatched giant screen showed pop videos at a volume that would have prevented conversation anyway.

Also, there was still a little alcove he recalled from his previous visits. A space where he could drink unseen, slowly medicating himself to dissipate his hangover. He took the first welcome swallow from his pint glass, then retrieved a crumpled copy of *The Times* from his pocket and turned to the crossword page.

Charles Paris, like many potential depressives, had a variety of methods for monitoring his mood. *The Times* crossword was one of them. Some days he would get the first clue instantly and fill in the rest of the grid with amazing fluency. Then he knew he felt good. Other days the clues could have been written in a foreign language, and while he scanned their impenetrable logic, he would become increasingly aware of his own inadequacies. The kind of person who couldn't even get a single clue in *The Times* crossword . . .

This day was a good one. He worked out a couple of answers in the top left of the grid straight away, and pretty soon had that whole quadrant filled. Then he slowed down a bit. He struggled with: 'Organ in action distributed (9)'. In the secret code known to all experienced solvers, 'distributed' could well be a signal for an anagram. And 'in action' did contain nine letters. So what anagrams were there of 'in action'? Charles wrote the letters out of sequence in a circle (one of the few habits he had learned from his father many years before) and studied them. Then realized that he'd counted wrong. There were only eight letters in 'in action'. So there was his anagram theory out of the window.

It was just as he had reached this conclusion that there was a lull between pop videos and he heard a male voice from the adjacent alcove saying, 'You were paid to keep your trap shut.'

The voice was rough London with an undercurrent of fastidiousness. Charles had never heard it before.

The voice that responded, however, was one he had heard, though he couldn't for the life of him remember where. Again male, it had an almost Bristolian burr as it said: 'Yes, but was I paid *enough* to keep my trap shut?'

The next music video started. Charles strained his ears against the pounding beat and managed to hear the first voice say, 'You accepted our terms when you agreed to do the job.'

'Maybe, but it strikes me now that the information I have might be worth rather more.'

'How do you mean?'

'Well, now the job's done, the stakes are higher.'

'I don't see that.'

'Then you're not thinking. Before the job was done, I had no power. I could say you'd asked me to do it. People might believe that, they might not – probably not, actually. But now the job has been done . . . I could generate some very bad publicity for you.'

'Not without incriminating yourself, you couldn't.'

'There are ways. I could also arrange some other accident to screw up your plans.'

'You're bluffing.'

'No, I'm not. If I don't get more money, you just wait and see what happens.'

There was silence. Not silence in the pub, obviously, but silence between the two men in the alcove next to Charles's. He strained his hearing even harder not to miss the restart of their conversation.

Finally, the London voice spoke. He did not get louder, but there was a fierce intensity to his words. 'If you try to black-mail us, you will live to regret it. Accidents, as you have reason to know well, can easily be arranged.'

That was a parting shot. So much so that it was immediately followed by the rattle and crash of the pub door closing. So Charles had no chance of discovering who had been making the threat.

He waited to see if the second man would follow immediately, but there was no sign of movement. Finding that his pint glass had unaccountably become empty, Charles Paris sauntered back to the bar to order a refill. Once there, he turned casually to check out the occupant of the alcove that the man with the London voice had just left.

It was the tall stagehand Bazza, who had been responsible for the logistics of getting the *Hamlet* skull set into the Grand Theatre, Marlborough. Which was interesting.

Bazza hadn't seen him, and Charles quickly rejected the idea of initiating contact with the man. The conversation he'd overheard had been intriguing, but capable of more than one interpretation. It wasn't the moment for Charles Paris to slip into amateur sleuth mode – not right there in The Pessimist's Arms, anyway.

He took his pint back to his own alcove. Where he realized that 'Organ in action distributed (9)' was definitely not an anagram. The 'organ' in question was a 'liver', the 'action' into which it was to be put was a 'deed', and so the solution had to be 'delivered'.

Charles Paris felt a warm glow.

The Tuesday night Dress Rehearsal didn't go on as long as the Tech, but it was still a late night. Charles Paris thought all the hard work had been worth it, though. The performance had inevitably been a stop-start affair, but replacing Jared Root with Sam Newton-Reid had totally transformed their production of *Hamlet*. The promise the boy had shown in that upstairs pub room was not illusory. Sam had genuine talent which could take him a long way in British theatre. He was also clearly intelligent. Charles found it a pleasure to hear Shakespeare's lines spoken by someone who understood their syntax, power and ambiguity.

And Sam's Nordic looks were perfect for the part. His pale wood-shaving eyelashes had been darkened with make-up. He looked wonderfully handsome and tortured, exactly as Hamlet should.

Charles Paris didn't have a dressing room to himself, but he was the last person left in his communal one and just contemplating whether to have a tot from his theatre bottle of Bell's or to wait till he got back to his digs bottle of Bell's, when he saw Sam Newton-Reid pass the doorway, arm-in-arm with Milly Henryson. They made an almost impossibly good-looking

couple. Charles felt an atavistic twinge of jealousy at the sight
of their youth and beauty. The girl's dark hair contrasted
wonderfully with her boyfriend's blond.

'Well done tonight,' Charles called out.

'Thanks. It was a bit of a baptism of fire,' the young actor
responded.

'Fancy a quick drink?' Charles didn't make the offer with
much conviction. No doubt Sam Newton-Reid was another of
the mineral water and gym generation.

But to his surprise the boy eagerly assented and then looked
slightly awkwardly at his girlfriend. 'It's all right,' said Charles.
'Milly is included in the invitation. Come in. I'm afraid it's
only whisky on offer. And no ice, unless someone's got the
energy to go down to the Green Room fridge.'

'Warm whisky'll be fine.' Sam sat down, and Charles could
see how much the strain of the day had taken out of him.
Milly looked at her boyfriend with a kind of anxious solici-
tude which made the older actor feel quite jealous. When
had a woman last looked at him like that? Charles was
reminded of his need for female company. Or yes, sex. Maybe
when the play opened, he'd be able to rearrange that drink
with Geraldine Romelle . . .?

'This is really good of you,' Sam Newton-Reid went on.
'I've been keeping myself together on the promise of a drink
at the end of the day and Milly's just broken the news to me
that she hasn't got any booze back at her digs.'

'Everything today has happened rather quickly,' the girl
apologized. 'I haven't had a moment to get to the shops.'

'Not your fault.' Sam took her hand. 'Just saying I was
desperate for a drink and didn't look like I was going to get
one, and now Charles has turned up like the Fairy Godmother.'

'Not a part I've actually played,' Charles confessed. 'Though
I have given my Baron Hardup.'

'Who's he?' asked Milly.

'Cinderella's father.' He remembered the pantomime in
Worthing way back in his career. And he remembered Jacqui,
who'd been playing a Villager, White Mouse and Court Lady
(for the Finale). They'd had a nice time during the run.

Unfortunately, though, he couldn't forget the review his

performance had received in the *Worthing Herald*: 'Charles Paris's Baron Hardup was particularly hard up for laughs.'

Feeling a little uneasy at being so much older than the young couple, Charles grinned and said, 'Great that you two get the chance to work together. Have you ever done so before?'

Milly Henryson looked a little piqued. 'Yes, we did quite a lot of stuff together at uni.' Charles didn't think he'd ever get used to people using the word 'uni' without irony. 'And then,' the girl went on, 'of course, more recently . . .'

She didn't finish the sentence, and Charles realized the proportions of the gaffe he just had made. The pub room production he had seen with Frances had not just featured Sam Newton-Reid in the title role. 'That is, Milly,' he mumbled, not making up nearly enough ground, 'apart from when you played Ophelia in that *Hamlet* I saw.'

'Well, as I say, we did do some stuff at uni.'

'Milly was brilliant in *Hedda Gabler*,' said Sam loyally. 'I played Tesman, but she totally stole the show.'

The girl's beautiful face wrinkled ruefully. 'Feels like a long time ago.'

Long time ago? echoed Charles's mind. You wait till you get to my age, love. Then you'll know what 'a long time ago' means.

Sam took his girlfriend's hand and shook it reassuringly. 'You'll get there, love. Remember, almost every great actor in this country has had to serve their time grafting away as an ASM at some point. Isn't that right, Charles?'

But before there was time for him to respond, Milly cut in with, 'You seem to have managed to avoid that stage, Sam.'

The exchange didn't qualify for the description of 'a spat', but it still showed an underlying tension in the young actors' relationship. Charles had never really had an affair with an actress where there had been professional rivalry, perhaps because his natural fatalism had prevented him from being too overt about his ambitions. But he did know many couples in the theatre for whom it had been a problem. Work patterns in their business were so erratic that the chances of both part-ners having exactly the same level of success at exactly the same time were distant. One career would be blooming while the other stagnated. One partner would be bathing in the glory and stimulus of nightly performances, while the other was stuck at home, enviously watching other actors who'd managed to get lucrative television work.

Charles had frequently seen the situation become a recipe for relationship breakdown. Because, of course, the more successful partner would be moving in more glamorous circles, possibly finding opportunities for new sexual adventures . . . He didn't for a moment believe that Sam Newton-Reid and Milly Henryson were currently at that level of risk, but he could recognize that the seeds of jealousy had been sown between them.

'Anyway,' said Sam, continuing his campaign of reassurance, 'there's a chance that we might work together again quite soon . . .' Milly grinned at him '. . . given the scale of Katrina's media commitments.'

Charles got it. He'd been aware during rehearsals of Katrina Selsey continually wanting to have a 'quick word' with Ned English at the breaks. He'd also seen the girl's Personal Manager Peri Maitland around the Grand Theatre and gathered that there had been many requests for time off so that Katrina could appear on chat shows and panel games. The other part of the equation, which he'd forgotten but had known at some point, was that Milly Henryson was understudying the role of Ophelia. So if there were a performance which Katrina Selsey's 'media commitments' prevented her from doing . . . then Milly would get to act with her boyfriend again.

'I should think it's quite likely you'd get on at some point during the tour, Milly,' said Charles.

'What makes you say that?'

'It's just that I wonder, even without her "media commitments", whether Katrina will have the stamina to do all the performances.'

'Oh?'

'She hasn't got a theatre background. Still really an amateur. She isn't used to the relentless grind of eight shows a week. I wouldn't be surprised if our Katrina doesn't call in sick at least once over the next week.'

Milly Henryson looked initially very excited by this idea,

then realizing it might make her appear to be willing the production's Ophelia to fall ill, she changed her expression to something more neutral.

Sam Newton-Reid turned to Charles, his brow wrinkled with ingenuous puzzlement. 'Milly's been telling me these amazing stories about Katrina Selsey's behaviour at rehearsals, some of which I just couldn't believe. I mean, is it true that she's been demanding chauffeured limousines to take her everywhere?'

'Well,' said Charles Paris judiciously, 'it's not a million miles from the truth.'

And if Sam Newton-Reid had been looking for a demonstration of the kind of behaviour Charles and Milly had been talking about, the next day, Wednesday, provided a perfect example. All three of them were in the auditorium of the Grand Theatre to witness it.

The rehearsal call was ten o'clock. Though they had made great strides the day before, integrating the new Hamlet into the production, a lot of hard work would still be required for the company to be ready for the first public performance the following evening.

There were warning signs in the fact that Katrina Selsey arrived glammed up to the nines. Not the usual sweatshirts, hoodies and jogging bottoms of rehearsal wear, but an impossibly short skirt, impossibly high heels, thick make-up and eyelashes like exotic moths. It was also ominous that she appeared accompanied by an equally well-dressed Peri Maitland.

Ned English's technical discussion with the designer in the stalls was interrupted by a peremptory call from Katrina onstage. 'Can we get started, please, and get my bits done? I've got to be away by eleven.'

'What?' asked a bewildered Ned.

Katrina Selsey looked to her Personal Manager to deal with the next bit. 'That's right,' said Peri Maitland. 'Katrina has to be away by eleven.'

'But we're rehearsing today,' said the confused director. 'And the bloody show's opening tomorrow night.'

'I'm sorry,' responded Peri Maitland, all sweet reasonableness. 'Katrina's got a telly recording.' She mentioned the name of a popular Friday night chat extravaganza, *The Johnnie Martin Show*. 'They pre-record on Thursday evening, which obviously she can't do because of the performance here, so they've agreed to do her segment separately. And today's the only day they'd got free.'

'They may be free,' said Ned English, finally rustling up some counter-arguments, 'but Katrina is not. She's committed to rehearsals here. Our schedule's already been knocked sideways by Jared's accident. We can't afford any more delays.'

'Listen,' said Peri, rather more forcefully, '*Johnnie Martin* is a very big deal. You can't argue with telly people.'

'You certainly can. Katrina is required to rehearse here this morning.'

'Why?' The actress herself rejoined the argument. 'I know all the lines and the moves . . .'

'That's not the point. There are other members of the cast who—'

'. . . and that girl, you know, the one who's understudying me, she can stand in for today's rehearsal.'

Katrina Selsey may not have been in show business very long, but she'd been quick to pick on certain aspects of star behaviour. Throughout the rehearsal period she'd made a point of pretending not to know Milly Henryson's name, referring to her always with the disparaging 'that girl'.

'I cannot rehearse without my full cast,' the director insisted.

'Listen, Ned,' said Katrina Selsey, a new Essex hardness in her voice, 'my appearance on national television on *The Johnnie Martin Show* on Friday night is going to do far more for this production of *Hamlet* than any amount of rehearsal.'

'She's right,' Peri Maitland chipped in. 'You can't buy that kind of publicity.'

'And,' Katrina went on, 'now Jared's out of the show we need something to get bums on seats. I'm the only star name left in this show.' A new thought struck her. 'And in fact, Ned, I should have Jared's dressing room.'

'For heaven's sake,' said the exasperated director. 'This

show opens tomorrow night. We haven't got time to talk about dressing rooms.'

'Well, we should,' insisted Katrina. 'And I should definitely have the star one. You don't think any of the other nonentities in the cast are going to bring the punters in, do you?'

Seated in the stalls, Charles Paris winced. And for once it wasn't from his hangover. For himself he didn't object that much to being categorized as a 'nonentity' (indeed, it chimed in with his self-image during his lowest moods). He didn't, however, think all the other members of the cast would be quite so forgiving.

But none of them said anything. They all just listened as the argument between stage and auditorium continued.

'Katrina's right,' Peri Maitland asserted once again. 'On Friday night this show will be known about by people who've never even heard of *Hamlet*.'

'That's as maybe,' said Ned English, 'but the fact remains that Katrina has signed a contract which means Tony Copeland Productions have first call on her services.'

'And suppose Tony himself feels it's more important that Katrina gets the telly exposure . . .?'

'I would think that is extremely unlikely.' Ned English's words sounded a little too defiant, as though he were afraid that Peri might be telling the truth.

The Personal Manager pressed home her advantage. 'Katrina's going to be giving a sneak preview of her debut single on *Johnnie Martin*. And Tony Copeland is a director of the company for whom she's recorded it.'

Charles Paris saw Ned about to question this and then think better of the idea. Peri Maitland could have been bluffing, but Tony Copeland's tentacles reached so far into so many areas of show business that her assertion could be true.

'Go on,' she continued, 'why don't you call Tony and ask him?' And she proffered her mobile phone towards the director.

Ned English was basically a weak man, and the way he backed off from the direct challenge was yet another demonstration of that weakness. 'Right,' he said, reaching for his script and calling out to the cast, 'let's make a start with the scenes involving Ophelia . . . *while we still have her services*.'

In spite of Ned's waspish final words, Charles Paris was left in no doubt that Katrina Selsey had won that particular battle. She left at eleven in a limousine sent by the company who made *The Johnnie Martin Show*. But, though she might have plenty on Facebook and Twitter, the victory certainly hadn't increased her number of friends in the *Hamlet* company.

NINE

Katrina Selsey was back in good time for the Wednesday evening Dress Rehearsal. Well before the 'half' (that moment thirty-five minutes before curtain-up by which all professional actors should have checked into the theatre). And she gave a good performance as Ophelia. Whatever criticisms might be made of her approach to other aspects of show business, none could be made of her application to her acting. She was serious about the profession and wanted to maximize her natural abilities. There would always have been something wooden about a performance by Jared Root, but not one by Katrina Selsey. Even those cast members who had been most offended by being called 'nonentities' had grudgingly to admit her talent.

Apparently, according to the Green Room grapevine, Tony Copeland had been in the audience for the Dress Rehearsal, but he did not come backstage afterwards. That evening was the first chance to get an impression of how long the show would run in normal performance. Charles was gratified to see that, from a seven thirty start, the last words of the play, *'Go, bid the soldiers shoot,'* were pronounced by Fortinbras at ten twenty. Ned English's cutting of the text had had the desired effect – there would be time to get to the pub before it closed! All was well in the world of Charles Paris.

He wasn't the only member of the company to take advantage of this opportunity, but he hadn't lost his old skills and was first to the bar, ordering 'a large Bell's with some ice' before anyone else had passed through the Stage Door. This being an evening – or at least half an hour – of social drinking, he had gone to the pub nearest to the theatre, a considerably more cheerful venue than the one he'd been to at lunchtime the previous day.

The landlord's attitude to licensing hours was commendably lax and Charles managed to fit in three doubles before time was called. He enjoyed the familiar banter of his fellow actors, inflated tales of disasters averted during the evening's performance. He was also glad to have confirmed that they weren't all of the mineral water and gym persuasion. Their presence comfortingly presaged more such post-show gatherings during the weeks of touring that lay ahead. Geraldine Romelle wasn't among the group, though, Charles noted wistfully. Where was she? Back alone in her digs with a bottle of Evian? Thinking about him? Unlikely.

The only slight damper to the actors' jollity came when first one, then another noticed that they'd received text messages from the Stage Manager. The whole company was to be in the auditorium at nine thirty the following morning for 'notes from Tony Copeland'.

There was some trepidation and taut laughter amongst the coffee- and mineral water-clutching cast as they sat facing the stage of the Grand Theatre on the Thursday morning. Nine thirty was an early call for a day which was scheduled to end with the first public performance of *Hamlet*. Not unprecedented – and their Equity representative would ensure they got the union-sanctioned breaks they were due during the day – but unusual enough to jangle their already overstretched nerves. And the mystique surrounding Tony Copeland did make him a rather frightening figure.

Charles Paris was one of the last to arrive. The previous night's session at the pub had enlivened rather than sedated him, so he'd needed a few more Bell's at his digs to get properly relaxed. He'd fallen asleep in his chair during some interminable catch-up of the current *Top Pop*, woken at three, lain wakeful till six and then overslept the alarm. At least it didn't matter that he hadn't shaved. He had a false beard for the Ghost (described in the play by Horatio as 'a sable silvered') and the First Gravedigger needed to be a bit stubbly.

He checked his watch as he bustled through the Stage Door. Nine twenty-seven. His parched brain cried out for coffee. Maybe there was a pot on in the Green Room . . .?

But he paused by the half-open door, immobilized by the sound of voices. The first was Katrina Selsey's. And she wasn't sounding like the demure, efficient Ophelia of the night before. More like a trader at Romford Market.

'Listen! I am your first priority! I am your only priority!'

'No, Katrina, that is not the case.' The voice was Peri Maitland's. She was used to keeping her cool – indeed, her job was based on keeping her cool – but her capacity to do so had clearly been tested by the preceding conversation. 'You are one of a series of clients for whom I'm responsible. And I cannot spend all my time looking after you.'

'But I'm going to be more famous than any of your other clients!'

'That may be so. It may not. Let's wait and see, shall we?'

'Look, Peri, Tony Copeland has appointed you to look after my interests. Do you want me to tell him that you're not doing all you should be?'

'Katrina, that is not an accurate assessment of the situation.' The Personal Manager's voice was studiedly cool, but the producer's name had bought a tremor to it. 'Tony Copeland employs Pridmore Baines, the company I work for, in many capacities. Managing you is just one of many contracts he has taken out with us. I've been assigned the task, but it is not exclusive. I have a long list of other clients who—'

'Let's see what Tony says about that!'

Charles Paris heard the voice getting louder as Katrina approached the door. Cheated of his coffee but not wishing to be caught eavesdropping, he scuttled out into the auditorium and sat at the back of the stalls. A moment later Katrina Selsey and Peri Maitland emerged to take their seats. From the expression on their faces no one would have known there'd been a word of dissension between them.

Charles noticed that Ned English was sitting in the auditorium with the cast, which was a measure of the director's insignificance in the scheme of things. Tony Copeland had made the nine thirty call, and Ned was as much in the dark about what was going to be said as the rest of the company.

Doug Haye from Tony Copeland Productions was also in the stalls, sitting at the end of a row, slightly back from the bulk of the company, watching the proceedings, as silent as ever.

On the dot of nine thirty Tony Copeland swept on to the stage. No chairs this time to give even a mildly casual air to the occasion.

'Good morning,' he said brusquely. 'I saw the Dress Rehearsal last night and was generally quite pleased with it. A few rough edges, but that's only to be expected with the last-minute change of cast. If you all concentrate and support Sam, *Hamlet* is certainly in a good enough state to open tonight.'

Such an announcement might in other circumstances have prompted comment or expressions of relief, but the assembled company remained silent. They all seemed to sense that Tony Copeland was simply sugaring the pill, that he had something else to tell them that would be less palatable.

'But the reason why I've called you all in this morning,' he went on, his tone confirming their fears, 'is in connection with publicity for the show. That's building nicely, and though I deeply regret what happened to Jared Root, it hasn't hurt in terms of column inches.' To Charles his words didn't sound callous, just pragmatic.

'However, it is important that you should all realize that the publicity for this show is being coordinated by Tony Copeland Productions *and no one else*! We set up the recording Katrina did yesterday for *The Johnnie Martin Show*.' His eyes focused on Ned English, sitting uncomfortably in the stalls. 'And I gather there was some problem with that.'

The director looked even more uncomfortable. 'I hadn't been told about it. I hadn't been told you had sanctioned it.'

'It was set up at the last minute. Some Hollywood sitcom bimbo dropped out of the Johnnie Martin line-up. We had to move fast.'

'Well, I didn't know that,' complained Ned petulantly. 'You could have told me.'

'From what I gather, Peri Maitland did tell you.'

'Yes, but I thought she was bluffing.'

'And why the hell should she be bluffing?' roared Tony Copeland. 'She told you to check with my office.'

'Yes, but—'

'Then why the hell didn't you?'

Ned English shrank into aggrieved silence. Charles Paris

tried to think of anything that might be more humiliating for a director than being bawled out in front of his full company, and couldn't come up with much. He looked across towards Katrina Selsey and Peri Maitland, both of whom were grinning broadly in self-congratulation.

'But,' Tony Copeland went on, 'that was not why I summoned you all here. As I said, all publicity for this show must be coordinated through the office of Tony Copeland Productions. And that applies to everyone. If you're approached by a journalist, by a television company, before you do anything you check it with my office.'

Charles Paris didn't think he'd have to bother much about this instruction. The chances of him being approached by a journalist or a television company were . . . well, 'minimal' was probably too strong a word.

'And what I say,' Tony Copeland pushed on, 'applies to every form of publicity – including social media. If any of you are thinking of putting anything about this show on Facebook or Twitter, you check it with my office first. I don't want my entire publicity campaign wrecked by a self-regarding actor posting some wanky comment.

'Do you understand that . . .' Tony Copeland swung round to face the culprit before saying the name '. . . *Katrina*?'

The smile of self-congratulation turned instantly to an embarrassed blush as the producer reached into his pocket for a mobile phone, clicked through to find what he wanted. 'There's a tweet I'd like you all to hear.' Flatly, he read out: '*Fab news! Got out of boring Hamlet rehearsals today to perform my new single on Johnnie Martin!*'

Tony Copeland's eyes skewered the unfortunate girl as he demanded, 'And do you think that is a responsible comment to post for the whole bloody world to see, Katrina? I'm spending a hell of a lot on publicity on this show, and it doesn't exactly help the campaign if one of the actors describes it as bloody boring!'

'But I wasn't saying the *show's* boring. I meant the rehearsals were—'

'Shut up! One more lapse of judgement like that, Katrina, and you'll be out of this show!'

'But I won *StarHunt*,' the girl insisted, trembling with emotion. 'You can't get rid of me!'

'You just watch me!' Tony Copeland snapped back. 'I can do what I bloody well like! I can cancel this whole show – now, this minute! Pull the plugs – like that!' He snapped his fingers. 'Or I can see how the tour goes, and if it's not up to scratch, I can cancel the West End transfer and fill the Richardson Theatre with the winners of this year's *Top Pop*. And don't any of you forget that!'

His eyes once again bored into the now weeping actress. 'Particularly you, Katrina. Never for a moment doubt who's in charge of this production.'

Charles Paris never had doubted it.

TEN

Productions of *Hamlet* vary as to where the director chooses to place the interval. Those doing the full text frequently follow the now old-fashioned custom of having two breaks, so as not to overstrain the bladders of the audience. For his trimmed-down version Ned English had followed the popular practice of breaking the play after Act IV Scene iv, which ends with Hamlet dragging off the newly murdered body of Polonius.

The general view among the company during the opening at the Grand Theatre Marlborough was that the first half had gone pretty well. The audience had been respectfully silent, seemingly caught up in the unravelling of Shakespeare's story. Nothing went wrong technically, the lighting in the recesses of the onstage cranium worked well, and when the house lights came up for the interval the applause was long and loud.

Charles Paris also reckoned that he had witnessed the emergence of a new star. Some actors, he knew, however good they were in rehearsal, only came alive in front of an audience. A few improved immeasurably in those circumstances, reaching heights of passion they had never reached before. And Charles reckoned Sam Newton-Reid was a member of that select band.

In the scene on the battlements that the Ghost and Hamlet shared, the boy was mesmerizing. After Charles had said the line, '*Revenge his foul and most unnatural murder,*' he had been electrified by the way Sam, tears glinting in his eyes, echoed the word: '*Murder!*'

And he found his own performance gaining new intensity as he responded,

> '*Murder most foul, as in the best it is,*
> *But this most foul, strange and unnatural.*'

It was an experience that had been rare in Charles Paris's varied theatrical career, but at that moment he felt he was in the presence of genius.

The Ghost in *Hamlet* is one of those parts which gives plenty of time for thumb-twiddling. The opening scenes are good, but you disappear after Act I Scene v, and have to wait around for your brief appearance in Geraldine's Closet Scene, Act III Scene iv. And that's it. Good part for getting to the pub early and getting well stocked-up before you stagger back on for the curtain call . . . unless, of course, you are also doubling the First Gravedigger, which throws such possibilities out of the window.

Later in the run Charles reckoned he'd get organized with a book or *The Times* crossword to fill the longueurs, but since it was the opening night, for the rest of the first half he drifted uneasily between his dressing room and the Green Room. The snatches of the play he heard on the tannoy and the comments of other actors confirmed his view that Sam Newton-Reid was giving an exceptional performance.

Charles could feel the heightened dramatic tension between Gertrude and Hamlet when he entered the Closet Scene. Just as he himself had when facing Sam Newton-Reid on the battlements, Geraldine Romelle was raising her game to match the young man's.

Charles Paris was so impressed that, though he'd never been one of those fulsome actors who spends all their time telling everyone they're 'mah-vellous', he did want to congratulate Sam during the interval. So, as soon as he heard the prolonged applause, he hurried along to the star dressing room.

A tap on the door produced no response. Sam Newton-Reid was probably held up by the congratulations of other cast members. But the door was ajar, so Charles pulled, expecting to find the room empty.

It wasn't empty. But there was no living thing in there. Katrina Selsey lay on the floor, a chair half-under her, as though she had backed away from something terrifying seen in the make-up mirror.

She was very still. The mascara was smudged about one red eye. But that wasn't as red as the blood that had soaked her blonde hair and pooled on the carpet around the back of her head.

ELEVEN

'Was Katrina Selsey popular with the other actors?' Charles was wary about how he should reply to that, so he resorted to the old trick of answering a question with a question. 'Why, are you suggesting she was murdered?'

'I'm not suggesting anything, Mr Paris. Merely trying to ascertain some facts, which will provide a background to the circumstances of her death.' Detective Inspector Shelley's manner was as formal as his language. It was impossible to know what he was thinking. He would have made a good poker player. Nor did the face of his sidekick, the female Detective Constable whose name Charles hadn't caught, give much away either.

It was the same evening, the Thursday. They were in Charles's communal dressing room, but the other actors had been sent home. The second half of *Hamlet* had been abandoned 'due to an accident to one of the cast', as the House Manager had told the audience with intriguing imprecision. The theatregoers had all gone home in a state of high curiosity. But the news of Katrina Selsey's death couldn't remain a secret for long. Actors thrive on gossip and have a very efficient grapevine for distributing it. In spite of Tony Copeland's strictures, Charles felt certain that some of the younger actors wouldn't have been able to restrain themselves from tweeting the news. It was only a matter of time before the Grand Theatre was once again besieged by journalists and television crews.

'So I revert to my question, Mr Paris. Was Katrina Selsey popular with the other actors?'

Charles was still determined to be cagey with his reply. He didn't know how much the detectives had heard from other company members. To give full details of Katrina's misdemeanours during rehearsal might at this stage be unwise. So all he said was, 'Everyone gets very tense running up to a

First Night. Nerves are frayed. People tend to snap at each other.'

'That's not really answering my question, Mr Paris.'

'No.'

'I've heard suggestions from other actors I've spoken to that Katrina Selsey was not the most popular person in the theatre.'

'Well . . .' Charles prevaricated. 'She came from a very different background from most of us. You know, she really had no experience as an actor. So she didn't know about . . . certain rules that most of us have, kind of, grown up with.'

'What kind of rules, Mr Paris?'

'Erm . . .' He couldn't really think of any that wouldn't highlight Katrina's unpopularity. 'Turning up on time to rehearsals, that kind of thing.'

'Are you saying she didn't turn up on time to rehearsals?'

'No.' In fact the girl had been extremely punctilious about that.

'What did you think of her, Mr Paris?'

Charles shrugged. 'She seemed to be a nice enough girl. Very inexperienced as an actress – actor.' He probably didn't need to make the correction for an audience of police officers, but it was best to be on the safe side with a woman in the room. You never knew when you were about to offend feminist sensibilities. 'I didn't know her that well,' he concluded limply.

'Did you like her?' This question came from the Detective Constable, and Charles caught something different in her tone from that of her male colleague. It was very definitely suspicion, and Charles remembered the old rule of crime fiction – and quite possibly crime fact: 'The first suspect is always the person who discovers the body.'

He tried not to change his tone of voice as he replied, 'I neither liked her nor disliked her. She was from a different generation, just someone I was working with. And not working with very closely. We weren't in any scenes together.'

'Did you spend any time with her socially?' Again it was the woman asking the question.

'I may have ended up in the same pub with her at the end of a day's rehearsal on a few occasions. But never just her and me on our own. Always with a lot of other people.'

'So if you didn't know her that well . . .' The Detective Inspector started the sentence, then smiled grimly and seemed to pass the conversational baton to his junior.

She instantly picked it up. '. . . why did you go to her dressing room during the interval of the play this evening?' Maybe this was some kind of Good Cop/Bad Cop routine that the two of them had rehearsed together many times before.

'I didn't know it was her dressing room.'

'Really?' There was a note of surprise, bordering on scepticism, in the Detective Constable's voice. 'But her belongings were all over it.'

'I only saw that when I went inside.'

'So whose dressing room did you think it was?'

'Sam Newton-Reid's.'

Detective Inspector Shelley consulted some handwritten notes. 'The actor who's playing Hamlet.'

'Yes.'

'And why did you want to see him?'

'He'd been stunningly good in the first half. I wanted to congratulate him.'

'Oh yes, of course. I dare say a lot of that kind of thing goes on in your profession.'

Charles bridled. He could sense the Inspector was within an inch of saying the word 'luvvie'.

'So why,' asked the Detective Constable, her voice again hardening, 'did you go to the wrong dressing room?'

'I didn't know it was the wrong dressing room. It's what's called the star dressing room.' Charles knew he was sounding flustered and as guilty as hell. 'So I assumed, since Hamlet is the ultimate star part, the actor playing Hamlet would be in the star dressing room. It was the dressing room that Jared Root had been in.'

'Ah yes, Jared Root,' Detective Inspector Shelley repeated thoughtfully and again looked at his notes. 'And it was the accident to him that led to Sam Newton-Reid being drafted into the cast?'

'Precisely, yes.'

'How did you get on with Jared Root, Mr Paris?' asked the Detective Constable, elaborately casual.

'Much as I did with Katrina Selsey. He was someone I was working with. Working more closely perhaps than I was with her.'

'Oh?' She picked this up as if it was some great revelation.

'Because,' Charles explained patiently, 'I was actually acting in scenes with him. The Ghost of Hamlet's Father, one of the parts I'm playing, appears to Hamlet on the battlements of Elsinore Castle. And the First Gravedigger, my other part, also has a scene with him. So I spent more time with Jared at rehearsal than I did with Katrina. But I didn't spend time with him socially,' he hastened to add before the question was asked.

'And what were your views, Mr Paris,' asked Detective Inspector Shelley, 'of Jared Root's abilities as an actor?'

'I don't see why that's relevant.'

'Oh, come on, you must have had views. Your opinion of Sam Newton-Reid's acting was so high that you wanted to congratulate him halfway through the performance. Did you think as highly of Jared Root's abilities?'

'No,' Charles admitted.

There was a satisfied silence between the two police officers, as though they had in some way scored a point. Detective Inspector Shelley again consulted his notes before saying, 'Did you believe that Jared Root's involvement in this production threatened its chances of success?'

'I don't see that that's relevant either to what we're talking about.'

'Ah, but what are we talking about, Mr Paris?' the Detective Inspector responded gnomically. 'We've only just met. We don't know each other. You might be talking about one thing, the Constable and I might be talking about something else entirely.'

There were a lot of sharp ripostes Charles Paris could have made to that, but sensibly he didn't voice any of them, just waited to see in which direction the next question would lead.

'What the Inspector was asking, Mr Paris,' said the Detective Constable, 'was whether you thought Jared Root's performance as Hamlet might jeopardize the chances of this play opening in the West End as planned?'

'It wouldn't matter what my view was about that. Such decisions are taken by the production company who're putting on the play.'

'But you must have had an opinion on the matter.'

'All right, I did . . . though my opinion would not have carried any weight in discussions about the subject. As someone who's been in this profession for a very long time, no, I didn't think that Jared Root had much talent when it came to acting. On the other hand, as a singer he apparently has a very big following among the younger generation. Tony Copeland, the producer of this show, is far from being a fool, and he believed Jared Root's appeal was strong enough to compensate for any shortcomings he might have had as an actor. So I have no reason to disbelieve him. And take my word for it, I've seen many actors with considerably less talent than Jared Root go on to have extremely successful careers in the theatre.'

'And is that something you feel bitter about?' asked the Detective Constable pointedly.

Charles Paris let out a weary sigh. 'No. I've been in this business far too long to bother getting bitter about things like that.'

There was another silence. Detective Inspector Shelley straightened up his sheets of notes and said, 'That will be all for now, Mr Paris. Thank you for your cooperation. We may need to speak to you again, but we have your mobile number and I assume we can contact you through the theatre.'

'Don't worry, I'm not about to leave the country.' The look on both of the police officers' faces made Charles regret his attempt at levity.

'And is there anything you'd like to ask us before you go?' asked the Inspector stonily.

'There are one or two questions, but I'm not sure that they're ones to which you're likely to give me answers.'

'Well, you can only find that out by asking them, can't you, Mr Paris?'

'All right.' Charles looked Detective Inspector Shelley

straight in the eye. 'Can you tell me what actually killed
Katrina Selsey?'

The reply was as formal as he would have anticipated. 'Until
a variety of examinations and tests have been conducted by
the appropriate police departments, it is impossible to answer
that.' Shelley returned his stare. 'Anything else?'

'Just one thing . . .' No harm in asking. 'Do you think there
is a connection between what happened to Jared Root and
Katrina Selsey's death?'

'Why?' demanded the Detective Constable. 'Do you, Mr
Paris?'

The press interest in Jared Root's accident had been as nothing
compared to the feeding frenzy over Katrina Selsey's demise.
Injury is never going to be as sexy as death. And the girl's
comparatively recent arrival in the public consciousness meant
that whatever she did was hot news. Also, she had been pretty,
and there's nothing the press likes better than a pretty victim
of an unexplained death. (None of the papers was yet using
the word 'murder', but without actually saying it they left the
obvious implication to be picked even by the least astute of
their readers.)

'Mystery death' was the expression favoured by the tabloid
editors to accompany their front-page pictures of Katrina
Selsey. This was a clever choice, because the word 'mystery'
could never fail to bring up a subliminal association with the
word 'murder'. At amazing speed, photographs were found of
her grieving parents, her grieving parents' house, the first
primary school Katrina had been to and her favourite Jack
Russell terrier, Justin. Tributes appeared from Tony Copeland,
Ned English and everyone else connected with the *StarHunt*
series. Senior figures from the world of show business who
felt they had been out of the spotlight too long gushed about
Katrina Selsey's exceptional talent and the tragedy of 'a great
career snuffed out so young'.

And, Charles was told by younger members of the cast, her
death was 'trending like mad on Twitter'. On hearing this, he
had done another of his sage, ignorance-hiding nods. Apparently,
they said, what had happened to Katrina totally eclipsed interest

in Jared Root's accident. Which would have cheered her enormously, had she been around to be cheered.

Sadly, no one in the *Hamlet* company seemed any better informed about how the unfortunate young woman had died than Charles Paris was. With the distinction of being the one who found the body, he was much questioned by his fellow actors about the exact circumstances of his discovery. And he was distressed to find how little he remembered.

As someone who had sometimes dabbled in a little light sleuthing, he chastised himself for not having shown more acuity at the crime scene. He should have lingered, assessed the situation, searched cold-bloodedly for clues. That's what any self-respecting amateur detective would have done. Whereas Charles Paris had been so shocked by what he saw that he'd immediately rushed out of the dressing room to find the stage management and get them to call for an ambulance.

During the next couple of days he frequently, when being questioned by other actors or just on his own, tried to focus, to bring back what he had actually seen. The blood pooled around Katrina Selsey's blonde head suggested she had received a blow from behind, but Charles hadn't had the temerity to move her to check out the wound. He knew how touchy the police could be about adulteration of crime scenes. Nor – as any Holmes or Poirot worth his salt would have done – had he examined the area for a bloodstained blunt instrument. Or recognized the distinctive aroma of a men's cologne only available from a little parfumerie on Andrássy Avenue in Budapest. Not for the first time, as a sleuth Charles Paris had been total rubbish.

The one detail that did stick with him from his sight of Katrina Selsey's corpse was that there had been something wrong with her right eye. A redness around the pupil and the mascara all smudged. It was a discordant image on a face whose make-up had always been so punctiliously perfect. As though she had rubbed fiercely at her eye shortly before she died. But for what reason she might have done that, Charles could only conjecture.

After the curtailed First Night, Tony Copeland's decision was texted to the cast the following morning. Because of all the confusion, not to mention out of respect for Katrina Selsey's memory, that night's performance would be cancelled. There would be rehearsals during the day to integrate Milly Henryson, Katrina's understudy, into the production, and the next performance of *Hamlet* for Marlborough's paying public would be the Saturday matinee.

As a result of this diktat, there was quite a lot of hanging around for the Grand Theatre company. Tony Copeland, afraid of indiscreet leaks to the press, had forbidden the cast from leaving the building until the end of the Friday's rehearsals.

And it was while he was idling in the Green Room, trying to bring his mind to bear on *The Times* crossword, that Charles Paris found the solution to one small mystery. Dennis Demetriades came in. That day the young man had no moustache but a centimetre-wide strip of beard outlining the lower contour of his jaw, a minimal Abraham Lincoln effect. Within minutes he and Charles were talking – inevitably – about Katrina Selsey.

'She was very determined,' said Dennis. 'When she wanted something, she just worried away until she got it.'

Charles agreed. 'Though I'm not sure she wanted what happened to her yesterday.'

'No. You haven't heard any more about what actually killed her . . .?'

Charles shook his head.

Dennis went on, 'If it turns out she was murdered . . . well, there'd be quite a few candidates to have done the job, wouldn't there?'

'You can say that again. Was there anyone in the company whose back she didn't manage to put up?'

Thoughtfully, Dennis Demetriades tapped his dark beard-fringed chin. 'Can't think of any offhand. I mean, it's the kind of behaviour you might expect from an established star . . .'

'Though I still think it's unforgivable, whoever's doing it.'

'Maybe, Charles.' Dennis didn't sound convinced. He was still new enough in the profession to be impressed by stories of stars' tantrums and impossible demands. 'But it certainly wasn't justified in Katrina's case. I mean, the rest of us . . . you know, the younger members of the cast . . . who've been through drama school and learnt a bit about discipline in the theatre . . . we were all appalled by the way she went on. The trouble is, kids from her generation, they think fame's just something that's given you on a plate. You don't have to work for it, you don't have to learn a craft – just suddenly one day you're famous. And that, they seem to think, gives them license to behave like total divas.'

Charles Paris suppressed a smile. If he'd heard that speech from one of his contemporaries, he wouldn't have been at all surprised – indeed, he *had* heard similar gripes from them more times than he cared to remember. But to hear it from an actor who had to be at most three years older than the girl he was talking about did seem a little incongruous. Not, of course, that Charles didn't agree with the sentiments.

'I mean, God,' Dennis Demetriades went on, 'that business about the dressing rooms . . .'

'Yes, I remember her going on to Ned about that at rehearsal. Though, for once, he seemed to assert himself and shut her up quite effectively.'

'You'd have thought so, wouldn't you? Most people would have said to themselves, "Look, you're not going to win on this one, ducky. You may think you're the most important person in this show, but the show in question is *Hamlet*, and if anyone has a right to the star dressing room in that play, then it has to be Hamlet." No argument. As I say, that's how most people would have seen it . . . but not our Katrina. Oh no.'

'Why, what did she do?' asked Charles.

'She waited till the First Night and staged a takeover.'

'What do you mean?'

'Like Hitler annexing the Sudetenland, Katrina just marched in and took over the star dressing room.'

'While Sam was onstage?'

'Yes. You know Ophelia has quite a big gap between Act II Scene i with Polonius, while Hamlet has all that stuff with Rosencrantz and Guildenstern and the Player King . . .'

'Till she has to come back on for the "Get thee to a nunnery" scene?'

'Exactly, Charles. Well, during that gap Katrina picked up the stuff from her dressing room and plonked it all in Sam's.'

'How do you know?'

'I saw her.' The young man realized he had said too much and looked suddenly evasive. 'I mean, I just happened to be passing along the corridor and I saw her carrying her things from her dressing room to Sam's.'

'Wow! She'd got some nerve, hadn't she?'

'Yes. I think she'd have been pretty safe, actually. Sam's not the sort to have made waves about something like that. Katrina knew she could have stood up to Ned English, and would Tony Copeland really have cared about a detail like who was in which dressing room?'

'Probably not.'

'Except, of course,' said Dennis Demetriades, his voice appropriately sombre, 'Katrina didn't get a chance to enjoy her triumph, did she?'

'No,' Charles agreed. 'Incidentally, one thing you said intrigued me . . .'

'Oh?'

'That image of Hitler annexing the Sudetenland.'

'Ah.' The young man reddened, anxious about having his credentials as a serious actor diminished. There were still a lot of people in the profession who regarded university graduates with suspicion. 'I trained at Rose Bruford. But before that,' he admitted sheepishly, 'I read History at Cambridge.'

Milly Henryson's performance as Ophelia was good. Charles, of course, had seen her in the role before, in the upstairs room of a Battersea pub, but she fitted well into the Grand Theatre show. Though she wasn't in any of his scenes (except in a coffin for the Gravediggers' – it was characteristic of a Ned English production that he insisted on an open coffin), the enforced idleness of the Friday meant that he sat in the auditorium and watched some of her rehearsals.

He reckoned Milly was better than Katrina Selsey had been in the role. She had a greater instinctive sense of stagecraft, she understood Shakespeare's language and spoke the verse more naturally. What's more, she didn't make suggestions like replacing the songs in the Mad Scene with ones off her latest album.

The basic difference lay in the fact that Milly Henryson was a professional actress (oh damn – actor). Katrina Selsey had had a deal of raw talent, but had her career developed, she would have moved more towards performing rather than acting – and Charles knew there was a big difference between the two. Winning the part of Ophelia in *StarHunt* might have kick-started Katrina's career, but her long-term future would have been in television presenting, being a 'personality', rather than in the theatre.

Milly Henryson, of course, looked absolutely wonderful on stage. Somehow her black hair and blue eyes suited a Jacobean setting. She was not very different in shape from Katrina Selsey, so the Ophelia costumes had needed the minimum of adjustment. And she looked particularly wonderful onstage with Sam Newton-Reid. The contrast between her dark colouring and his blondness brought something extra to their scenes together. The pair looked even more beautiful onstage than off.

From his vantage point in the stalls, Charles Paris quickly came to the conclusion, though, that their talents were not equally matched. The star quality that Sam Newton-Reid had was something which his girlfriend would never share. Though Milly Henryson might have a successful career in the theatre – given her looks, probably a very successful one – she would never be as remarkable as Sam.

But they clearly loved working together. Seeing them in rehearsal, teasing out the meanings of lines, adjusting to each other's performances, Charles could see that they were enjoying the reality of a long-held dream.

And Milly, of course, was a much less disruptive figure in the company than her deceased predecessor had been. From the point of view of the Tony Copeland Productions' *Hamlet*, both pieces of recasting had been bonuses.

Milly Henryson was ecstatic to be playing Ophelia. There was a buzz about her right through the Friday's rehearsals. Some of it was just sheer euphoria, but Charles Paris could detect another quality in her behaviour. Could it be an air of triumph?

TWELVE

The scenes featuring Ophelia in the Saturday matinee of *Hamlet* at the Grand Theatre Marlborough were a little tentative, but by the evening Milly Henryson had overcome her nerves and the general view among all the cast was that they had given their best performance yet. So a large number of the company (though not, Charles noticed with regret, Geraldine Romelle) adjourned to the nearest pub to celebrate. Again the landlord's relaxed approach to the licensing hours allowed them to fit in an hour's drinking.

When time was finally called, Charles Paris floated from the pub to the bottle of Bell's in his digs. As he sat in front of the television, cradling a glass and watching yet another catch-up on the progress of the current *Top Pop* series, he started to feel maudlin. Plaintive words formed in his mind. *Where have you gone, Geraldine? Where is it you go after every rehearsal, every performance? Why don't you join me here? We'd really get on, you know.*

He woke cold and cramped at a quarter to four, staggered to his bed and managed a few more sweaty, restless hours of sleep.

He didn't feel good when he woke at quarter to nine. Thank God, he thought, that the place where he was staying was self-catering. The idea of facing a landlady over breakfast was more than he could bring himself to contemplate.

On the other hand, 'self-catering' did carry with it the implication that he should cater for himself. And he hadn't got in much in the way of supplies. Except for the bottle of Bell's . . . which bizarrely seemed overnight to have emptied itself.

Charles Paris felt grouchy and self-pitying. Eating something, he knew, would help, and he was sure Marlborough must boast cafés that would be open on a Sunday morning – indeed, he'd seen a plethora of them along the High Street. And yet the thought of sitting in public and . . .

The pubs would be open at twelve, no doubt offering deals on Sunday Roasts. And after a few drinks he'd be able to eat more easily. But twelve o'clock seemed an awfully long way away.

A shower would help. Stop him feeling so sweaty, at least; get rid of the sense of dampness around the collar of the shirt he'd slept in.

But no. First he needed to ring Frances.

Yes, of course. Once he'd had the idea, he couldn't think why he hadn't had it earlier.

Frances would cheer him up. She was still his wife, after all. And she'd be free, no school on a Sunday. Charles knew there hadn't been a railway station in Marlborough since the Lord Beeching cuts of the 1960s. But he could get a cab to Swindon, then the train from there to London only took about an hour. He and Frances could meet for lunch. Or maybe she'd cook for him. Wow, Sunday lunch with his wife – how nostalgic would that be?

Alternatively, she might offer to drive down to join him for lunch in Marlborough. They'd find a nice pub – there were plenty of those, they weren't all like The Pessimist's Arms – then, boozed-up and randy, they'd come back to his digs.

Her number was in the memory of his mobile. Some silly psychological block – or perhaps his natural innumeracy exacerbated by age – prevented him from remembering what he still thought of as her 'new' number. Though it was many years since Frances had moved from the house they'd shared into a flat.

He pressed the relevant keys to call her. The ringing tone went on. And on. She must be out. He was about to ring off when the call was picked up. 'Hello?' Frances's voice was muzzy and a bit resentful. Oh shit, he'd woken her up.

'Um, it's . . . er, Charles.'

'Why?'

'What do you mean – why?'

'Why are you ringing me now?'

'Well, er . . .'

'You know how knackered I get during the week. I thought you might have remembered how much I count on my lie-in on a Sunday.'

He did remember now. He also remembered sharing those lie-ins with. Waking slowly to lazy, unhurried fondling and . . .

'What do you want, Charles?'

'I just . . . I just wanted to hear your voice.' As he said the words, he knew how corny they sounded.

'Don't be trite. Look, if there's something you want to say, say it quickly and then there's a chance I might be able to get back to sleep. I got to bed very late last night.'

Why? What were you doing? And with whom? But fortunately Charles managed not to vocalise the questions.

'Well, Frances, I just . . . wondered what you were doing today?'

'I cannot begin to imagine why it's of any interest to you, but I have a lunch date. And if that's all you wanted to ask me—'

'No, I was just thinking it'd be nice if—'

'Goodbye, Charles.'

God, what an idiot he was. Why on earth had he rung her? He had hoped for reassurance from the call, but all it had done was to unsettle him. Also to make him jealous. Who had Frances been with last night, the person who had kept her up so late? And who was her 'lunch date' with? He knew the younger generation used the word 'date' in any number of contexts – 'play date', 'spa date' and so on. But when someone of Frances's generation said 'lunch date' surely there was some overtone of a romantic assignation . . .?

The knowledge that he had long ago forfeited any rights to know anything about his wife's love-life didn't make him feel any better.

Miserably, grabbing a grubby towel, Charles Paris made his way towards the shower.

The weekend didn't improve. Many of the *Hamlet* company had taken the opportunity of a day and a half free to visit friends and lovers in London, where no doubt they would gossip with more speculation than information about Katrina Selsey's death. But there were probably a few still around Marlborough. Charles had the contact sheet the stage management had given to all the cast; he could easily call someone to see if they were free for lunch. What might Geraldine Romelle be doing, he wondered wistfully.

But he didn't make any calls. His loneliness was too deep to want company. Instead, to chime in with his mood, on the dot of twelve he pitched up at The Pessimist's Arms. After a couple of pints by way of rehydration, he ordered a glass of red wine to accompany his gristly beef and leathery Yorkshire Pudding. When he went up to order his third red wine, the barman told him unhelpfully that it would have been cheaper to buy a bottle.

More solitary drinking took place on the Sunday evening and Monday lunchtime. At that evening's performance of *Hamlet*, the Ghost of Hamlet's Father and the First Gravedigger both stumbled over a few of their lines.

Charles Paris was woken on the Tuesday morning by a call on his mobile. The move he made to sit up and answer it was far too sudden. His head felt as though steel knitting needles were being pushed into it from a variety of angles.

'Good morning, is that Mr Paris?'

'Er, yes.'

'This is Detective Constable Whittam.' A female voice. So the surname he didn't catch during his Good Cop/Bad Cop interview in his dressing room was 'Whittam'.

'Oh, good morning. How can I help you?' He knew his voice sounded unnatural, overeager to please. Why was it that he always felt guilty in the face of authority figures?

'I just wanted to check something about the evening of Katrina Selsey's death.'

'Fine. Check away,' said Charles, clumsily insouciant.

'You remember we talked about your visit to what you called "the star dressing room"?'

'Yes.'

'And you said that you weren't expecting to find Katrina Selsey in there?'

'That's right.'

'Well, from what we've heard from Mr Newton-Reid, it seems that she only moved into the dressing room during the performance that evening, just before her death.'

'Really?' Confirming what Dennis Demetriades had told him. But Charles didn't volunteer that information. He'd wait to see which way the questioning was leading.

'I just wondered whether you knew that, Mr Paris?'

'I've already told you I didn't. But you say that Sam Newton-Reid did?'

'Well, he kind of deduced it. He had been using it as his dressing room at the beginning of the performance . . . you know, he had changed into his costume there, then left it when the play started and wouldn't have got back there till the interval.'

'No, Hamlet's one of those parts that doesn't give you much opportunity to loll about in your dressing room.'

'And, of course, he never did get back to the dressing room because by then you'd discovered Katrina Selsey's body . . .'

'And the place was a crime scene.'

'The scene of an unexplained death,' Detective Constable Whittam corrected him formally.

'Of course. So Sam didn't actually *know* she was planning to take over his dressing room?'

'Not before it happened, no. Why do you ask, Mr Paris?'

'Well, I was just wondering whether there's some other explanation for why Katrina moved her stuff.'

'What explanation?'

'I don't know. I was just exploring the possibilities.'

'We know that Katrina Selsey had announced her intention to take over the dressing room.'

'Really? Who did you hear that from?'

'Her Personal Manager. Peri Maitland.'

Instantly, suspicion blossomed in Charles's mind. 'Was she with Katrina when the move actually took place?'

'No. She told us she caught a train from Swindon back to London that evening before the performance started. But as Peri Maitland was leaving the theatre Katrina Selsey told her what she planned to do.'

'Didn't Peri try to dissuade her?'

'I asked the same question, Mr Paris. Peri Maitland said that she had given up arguing with Katrina Selsey. I got the impression the girl was a client she wouldn't be sorry to lose.'

'Hm.'

'So, Mr Paris, we know what Katrina Selsey intended to do, but we don't have a witness who saw her actually doing it. I was wondering whether perhaps another actor might have been backstage and seen her taking her belongings into the star dressing room . . .?'

Something told Charles to be cautious. It was possible that the police hadn't questioned Dennis Demetriades. But if they had and the young man, for reasons of his own, had not revealed what he had seen, then Charles didn't want to land him in it. 'Someone may have done,' he said, 'but no one's mentioned it to me.'

'Really?' Detective Constable Whittam sounded disappointed.

'Have you asked the rest of the company about it? Because, as you say, someone may have seen—'

'We've asked them.'

'Ah.'

'Obviously. Because, of course, it would be very helpful if we had a witness to her entrance into the dressing room.'

'I can see that. Then you'd know whether she had gone in on her own or with someone.'

'Who did you have in mind?'

'Well, whoever it was who murdered her.'

'This is not a murder enquiry, Mr Paris. We are still awaiting forensic reports on what killed Katrina Selsey.'

The frostiness in her voice certainly put him in his place. He waited, tense for the next direction of her interrogation, but all Detective Constable Whittam said was, 'Thank you very much for your time. Goodbye, Mr Paris.'

'Goodbye.'

The call left him thoughtful. If, as she said they had been, all of the rest of the company had been asked the same question, then why had Dennis Demetriades been unwilling to tell the police what he had so readily told his fellow actor? Did the young man have something to hide?

Dressed as the Ghost, his false beard 'a sable silvered', Charles Paris came offstage at the end of Act I Scene v with Sam Newton-Reid's words ringing in his ears.

'The time is out of joint. O, cursed spite,
That ever I was born to set it right!'

Charles wandered through to the Green Room in search of coffee. He still felt ropey, but was determined not to let tonight's performance be as bad as the previous day's. He hadn't fluffed any lines in his first scenes. An injection of caffeine might help hold him together for the rest of the evening.

Serendipitously, there was only one other person in the Green Room. Dennis Demetriades, busy as ever with the buttons of his mobile.

No time like the present, thought Charles. 'I had a call today from Detective Constable Whittam.'

'Oh yes?' The young man looked up from the phone, his dark eyes wary.

'She said she'd talked to everyone in the company . . .'

'So?'

'. . . which I assume includes you?'

'I had a call from her, yes.'

'She told me she'd asked everyone if they'd seen Katrina Selsey moving dressing rooms . . .'

'Ah.' If Dennis Demetriades hadn't worked out before where Charles's questions were leading, he knew now. But he didn't volunteer anything, just waited.

'And nobody had. Which rather surprised me. Given what you told me the other day.'

'Yes.' The young man looked confused and conflicted.

'Why did you lie to the Detective Constable, Dennis?'

'I didn't want anyone to know I was up on that floor, you know, where the star dressing room is.'

'When you say "anyone", are you talking about the police?'

'Well, partly them, but, even more, people in the company.'

'Oh? You realize this does make your behaviour seem rather suspicious, Dennis.'

'Yes, yes, I can see that.' Now it was Charles who waited. Finally, the young man went on, 'Look, the fact is that my dressing room is on the basement level.'

'I know.'

'So I might come up to the ground floor to go to the Green Room or onstage, but there's no real reason for me to go up to the floors above.'

'Exactly. So why did you on Thursday night?'

Dennis Demetriades looked very cowed. Charles Paris reckoned his Ghost of Hamlet's Father costume was helping. There would be something awe-inspiring for most people about being interrogated by an avenging spirit in full armour.

'I . . . Look, the fact is, Charles . . . Up at the top of the theatre there's a kind of attic floor.'

'Oh?'

'Yeah. No one goes up there much. It's used as a kind of store room, full of old props, broken bits of sets. Some of it been there for decades, you know the kind of stuff.'

'Yes.'

'Well, since we've been here, I've kind of got in the habit of going up there . . .'

'Why?' Charles's mind flooded with possibilities. Was Dennis Demetriades using the attic as a kind of love nest, an impromptu knocking-shop? And if so, who was he knocking? Was it possible that he and Katrina had had a sexual thing going on?

This flow of conjecture was quickly stemmed as the young actor said, 'Fact is, I tend to go up there for a smoke.'

'A smoke?'

'Yes. As we keep being told, the Grand Theatre is a "non-smoking" building. We're not allowed to go outside in costume, so the Stage Doorman'd see me if I went out the back. And there's no way I can get through the whole of *Hamlet* without a smoke.'

'When you say "smoke",' hazarded Charles, 'are we talking "wacky baccy"? Cannabis? Pot?' He was uncertain what term the younger generation might use.

Dennis Demetriades looked affronted at the suggestion. 'No, just an ordinary roll-up.'

The more he thought about it, the more Charles believed the explanation. Fortunately, he'd never got into cigarettes, but, as a practising alcoholic, he could still empathize with the resentment of smokers at the increasing nanny-state restrictions of their pleasures. Dennis Demetriades hadn't been worried about the police knowing of his clandestine smoking room; he was afraid of some self-righteous, mineral-water-swigging, gym-frequenting member of the *Hamlet* company finding out about it. And then grassing him up to the Company Manager. His reason for keeping quiet on the subject to Detective Constable Whittam made perfect sense.

Charles Paris grinned. 'Don't worry, Dennis. Your secret is safe with me.'

The young man grinned back.

'But what you told me before was true? You did see Katrina moving her stuff into Sam's dressing room?'

'You betcha. I saw both of them.'

'Both of them?'

'Katrina was with that Personal Manager of hers . . .'

'Peri Maitland?'

'Yes. Peri was helping carry things.'

THIRTEEN

I t was perhaps symptomatic of Charles Paris's career that he didn't receive one of Peri Maitland's business cards. The Personal Manager had sprayed them around lavishly at the *Hamlet* read-through and during subsequent encounters with the company, giving a card to anyone who might need to make contact about Katrina Selsey's career, anyone who might at some stage, in some circumstances, be important. Charles didn't qualify.

He didn't have any difficulty finding one, though. Peri, whose entire business as a public relations consultant was predicated on her being instantly contactable, had thoughtfully pinned a card up on the Green Room noticeboard.

Charles copied down her number on a scrap of paper. Calling her straight away was not an option. When dressed in full armour as the Ghost of Hamlet's Father he tended not to carry his mobile.

In fact he didn't want to contact Peri Maitland straight away. He tried to persuade himself he didn't need to contact her at all. So, Katrina Selsey's Personal Manager had lied about when she left the Grand Theatre, which train she had got from Swindon back to London. She no doubt had reasons of her own for doing that. Did those reasons have anything to do with Charles Paris?

Dennis Demetriades had also lied to the police, but Charles wasn't about to expose him to Detective Constable Whittam. Nor did he particularly want to get Peri Maitland into trouble. He couldn't help being intrigued, though. If he hadn't been the one who found Katrina Selsey's body he might not have cared. But somehow that unhappy discovery made him feel inextricably caught up in the investigation of her death. Charles couldn't detach himself. He needed to find out anything there was to be found out.

Don't do anything till the interval, he decided. The Ghost

of Hamlet's Father still had his appearance to make in Gertrude's closet, and he'd feel a fool putting in a call to Peri Maitland in full armour. Maybe he'd wait till after he'd played both his parts, till he'd finished his stint as the First Gravedigger. But even as he had the thought he knew he was just procrastinating. If he waited till the end of the evening he wouldn't phone Peri; he'd convince himself he'd left it too late. No, if the deed were going to be done, it should be between his exit as the Ghost and his entrance as the Gravedigger.

One decision made, Charles was faced by another uncertainty. Was phoning Peri Maitland actually going to be the best way of contacting her? If he got through, identified himself and she didn't want to talk to him, it could be a very short conversation. He didn't really have any firepower, or threats with which he could keep her on the line. The only advantage he did have was private knowledge, the information he'd been given by Dennis Demetriades. But he didn't want to tell her that straight away.

While he was mulling this over, the interval came and the dressing room was suddenly full. All the young actors who shared with him immediately started doing what all young actors did at any break during rehearsal or performance: getting out their phones and texting.

Texting? Charles didn't do it much. He knew how to, but he found the process very laborious and cumbersome. His fingers felt too big for the tiny keys. On the rare occasions he did send a text, it took ages, holding the phone with one hand while a single finger of the other pecked away at the keyboard, making frequent mistakes, constantly having to delete and rewrite, getting confused by the outlandish suggestions thrown up by predictive text. He struggled . . . while the younger generation seemed to rattle away two-handed with the ease of an infinite number of monkeys typing up the *Complete Works* of Shakespeare.

Particularly the girls. When they were texting, their fingers were just a blur in front of the screens of their phones. Maybe, Charles wondered, it was because they tended to have longer fingernails. Yes, longer, pointy fingernails painted in garish colours must limit the number of errors and make the whole process much simpler.

On the other hand, when he thought about it, despite the deficiency of his skills he could see the advantages of texting Peri Maitland. The main one was that he felt pretty certain she didn't know his mobile number and wouldn't be able to guess who the text had come from. Which, if he phrased the message right, would be an advantage.

He did the deed straight after the interval. The dressing room had emptied again as the other actors got ready to swell the ranks of Fortinbras's army in Act IV Scene iv. Charles Paris had got out of his Ghost of Hamlet's Father kit. The armour wasn't all actually metal, thank God, except for the helmet, a mighty coal scuttle with a lot of interior padding. But the chain mail (silver-painted knitted tunic and leggings), small bendy bits (silver-painted leather) and big rigid sections like the breast-plate, vambraces, greaves, etc. (fibreglass) still made it a lot to lug around for any length of time. It was a costume he always removed with some relief.

He hadn't yet donned the muddy habiliments of the First Gravedigger, but sat cooling himself in just his black briefs. (Charles Paris hadn't ever made the move to boxer shorts; he liked to feel that everything was nice and secure under his clothes.)

So, nearly naked, he composed his text to Peri Maitland, not straight on to the phone, but with a pen on the back of an old rehearsal schedule. He did it very slowly, wanting to get the wording exactly right. What he came up with, after considerable rewriting, was: 'I HEAR THAT YOU HELPED KATRINA MOVE HER STUFF INTO THE STAR DRESSING ROOM THE NIGHT SHE DIED. IF YOU'D LIKE TO TALK ABOUT IT, CALL THIS NUMBER.'

He was quite pleased with what he'd done, but still not convinced he'd got the tone right. He didn't want to sound too threatening. The suspicion that Peri Maitland might have killed Katrina Selsey had not entered his head. But he felt sure the Personal Manager knew more about the circumstances of the girl's death than he did. He was after information. All he wanted from his message to Peri was that it should prompt her to call him back.

Charles knew he wasn't going to improve on the wording,

but still he dithered. What would he say if Peri Maitland did
ring back? Slowly, deliberately, he keyed the message into his
mobile. Copying from the scrap of paper he'd found in the
Green Room, he entered her number. Then, again, he started
to get cold feet.

It was the low mumbling from the dressing room tannoy
that forced him to act. There was singing from onstage. Charles
turned up the volume to hear, in Milly Henryson's pure soprano:

> '*Let in the maid, that out a maid*
> *Never departed more.*'

Near the end of the Mad Scene. Time he got into his First
Gravedigger outfit.

He pressed the 'send' button on the phone. Even as he did
it, part of him hoped that he'd copied Peri Maitland's number
wrong, or that some technical glitch would divert the text from
its destination.

But the deed was done. He felt his way into the First
Gravedigger's grubby smock.

At the end of the show Charles Paris found himself going
towards the Stage Door with Geraldine Romelle. 'Oh, we
talked about having a drink together one evening, didn't we?'
He pitched the words incredibly casually, as if the original
suggestion had been of little moment, and hadn't gained much
more moment in the intervening days.

'So we did,' said Geraldine. 'But then life – or rather death
– intervened, didn't it?'

'Yes. Mind you, as a plan, I think it had quite a lot going
for it.' Still keeping it all very light, he consulted his watch.
'We've actually got time to have a drink now.'

'Have we?'

'Yes,' said Charles, so laid back he was almost falling over.
'What would you say to the idea?'

'Why not?' said Geraldine Romelle.

Since she wasn't one of the regular post-show pub-goers,
Geraldine wasn't aware that Charles didn't take her to the

closest one, where other members of the *Hamlet* company might be encountered. He didn't want to depress her totally by taking her to The Pessimist's Arms, but there was another small cosy hostelry just off the High Street, a couple of roads away from the Grand Theatre's Stage Door.

Geraldine said she'd like a red wine, so Charles decided he'd join her and came back from the bar from a bottle of Chilean Cabernet Sauvignon and two glasses. She did the smallest of eyebrow-raises. 'You'll have to drink more of that than I will.'

'I'll force myself,' said Charles as he sat in the alcove opposite her and filled the glasses.

'I can't stay long,' said Geraldine Romelle.

'No problem. It'll be closing time in half an hour, so they'll kick us out, anyway.' He thought, but didn't say, *And if you were to fancy another drink you could come back to my digs.*

He raised his glass and they clinked. 'Felt like a good show tonight.'

She nodded. 'Yes, it's settling down.'

'Had quite a lot to settle down from.'

'You can say that again. Still, it's an ill wind . . .'

'Meaning what, Geraldine?'

'Meaning that, while wishing the accidents to Jared and Katrina hadn't happened, we have ended up with a considerably better show.'

'Yes. Sam's a real talent, isn't he?'

A vigorous nod. 'The real thing. He's electrifying in the Closet Scene. Don't see that very often.'

'And Milly . . .?'

'Good. Good enough. And you do see that quite often.'

'So you think Sam'll get to the top, and she'll be left trailing and flailing in his wake?'

Geraldine Romelle shrugged. 'Who knows? As I'm sure you realized long ago, Charles, talent is only a small part of it in this business. It's getting the breaks and . . .'

'That sounded rather heartfelt.'

'Not particularly. Oh, I see what you mean. Was I bemoaning the fact that in my career I hadn't got the breaks?'

'Well, I . . .'

'It genuinely doesn't bother me, Charles. Sure, everyone'd like to be hailed as the greatest thing since Sarah Bernhardt. And we'd all like to have a bit of the money that goes with star status.'

'Or a nice juicy television series that sells around the world?'

'Hm. I've never much enjoyed working in television.'

'One can put up with a lot for the kind of money they pay.'

'Maybe. Though, in my experience, every time I've started out on a job thinking, "Wow, the money's good," I've ended up earning every penny and just desperate for it to finish.'

Charles nodded. 'I know what you mean.' Then he mused, 'That's an expression that would never be heard from anyone involved in a Tony Copeland production . . .'

'What expression?'

'"Wow, the money's good."'

Geraldine Romelle giggled. She had very straight teeth, white but not whitened. Somehow that comforted Charles; it made him feel she was part of his generation. The generation that still had naturally coloured teeth. 'You're right,' she said. 'I mentioned to a friend that this show might be going to the West End and he said, "You'll clean up there." Then I told him Tony Copeland was producing and he immediately changed his tune.'

'You said "might be going to the West End". I thought that was kind of written into the contracts.'

'Charles, Charles, don't be naive. *Options* are written into the contracts, not guarantees. Surely you've been around long enough to know that.'

'Yes, of course I have, but—'

'I never believe anything in this business until it's happened. Find that approach saves a lot of heartache.'

'Yes, I'm normally like that. But Tony Copeland has talked very positively since day one about the show going in.'

'On day one it starred Jared Root from *Top Pop* and Katrina Selsey from *StarHunt*. Now we've got Sam Newton-Reid and Milly Henryson from nowhere.'

'They're much better actors.'

'That's not the point. Who is there in the cast now who's going to put Tony Copeland's demographically young bums on seats? You, Charles? Me? I don't think so.'

He grinned ruefully. Of course she was right.

'And first and foremost Tony Copeland's a businessman. He'll pull the plugs on this *Hamlet* without a second thought if he doesn't think he's going to make a profit.'

'But surely he's got the Richardson Theatre booked?'

'I'm sure it's just another option, Charles. Which he can take up or drop as he wishes. Or he can kill *Hamlet* after the tour and put in something else. What – a line-up of singing wannabes from the latest series of *Top Pop*? It wouldn't be out of character for Tony Copeland.'

Charles Paris liked Geraldine Romelle. Her cynicism about – and love for – the theatre matched his own. Sitting opposite, he was again struck by how dishy she was. The copper-coloured hair was tight against her head, not yet having got its bounce back after the hours it had been constrained under Gertrude's wig. She had scraped off her stage make-up and only replaced a neat dab of pale lipstick.

But Charles had never before been close enough to see what astonishing eyes she had. On forms they'd probably be written down as 'hazel', but that was an inadequate description of the multifaceted flecks of colour they contained. There were glints of gold in there, which made Charles think of Gustav Klimt paintings.

Geraldine Romelle's body was trim and toned. The discreet cleavage revealed by her open-necked shirt promised firmness and infinite speculation.

She was aware of his scrutiny and gave a smile which both excited and embarrassed him.

'Anyway,' she said, picking up the conversation, 'anyone who goes into the theatre for the money needs their brain testing. It's certainly not what drew me into it.'

'So what did?'

'I love acting,' she replied simply. 'It intrigues me. Or perhaps I should say that human nature intrigues me, and acting is a wonderful way of exploring it. That's another reason why I don't enjoy television. It's all done too quickly – particularly these days. You used to get a bit of rehearsal, now they just let the cameras roll. Which is why so many television actors can only do one thing. Simple for the director.

Whenever he turns the camera on them he knows exactly what performance he's going to get. So when you're acting in that kind of set-up you fall back on technique rather than genuinely trying to get inside a character's mind. I like the rehearsal process, the slow excavation of the person the playwright's created. That's what gives me a buzz. Don't you feel it too?'

Charles Paris's protective layer of cynicism had been hardened over so many years that he normally avoided discussions about how acting worked. It was a subject that attracted a great deal of vacuous pretension and bullshit, the kind of stuff that was regularly pilloried in the *Private Eye* 'Luvvie' column. But, transfixed by Geraldine Romelle's amazing eyes, he couldn't help admitting that he too got a buzz out of discovering the depths of a character.

Somehow they'd got through most of the Cabernet Sauvignon. Charles divided the last dribbles equally between them. 'You see. I didn't end up drinking most of it.'

'No, I seem to have kept pace with you pretty well, don't I?' Geraldine looked at her glass a little wistfully. 'Perverse, isn't it, how one bottle never seems quite enough. But sadly, they've called time, so there's nothing we can do about it.'

Charles was about to say that he had a very good idea of something they could do about it, when his mobile rang. 'Excuse me, Geraldine, I'd better take this.'

'Sure.'

He pressed the relevant button and heard, 'This is Peri Maitland.'

'Just take it outside. Won't be a moment. Don't go.'

He scuttled outside as he heard Peri asking, 'Who is this I'm talking to?' Her voice retained the professional poise of a public relations consultant, but there was an underlying tension there too.

'Who are you?' she asked again.

'Charles Paris.'

'Ah.' There was a silence as she assessed this information. 'And I have got the right number? Did you send me a text about the night Katrina . . .?'

'Yes.'

'I've been at one of my client's concerts at the O2 and only just switched on my phone.'

'Right,' responded Charles, still uncertain which way she was going to jump.

'We need to talk,' said Peri Maitland.

'Isn't that what we are doing?'

'Face to face. I could get up to Marlborough tomorrow morning. Would you be free to meet about twelve?'

'Yes.'

'I'll text you in the morning with the venue.'

Charles was aware of Geraldine Romelle emerging from the pub. 'Right, but could you just—?'

The line went dead.

Geraldine touched him on the arm. 'Thanks for the drink, Charles. I must be off.'

'Oh, but I was thinking we—'

'See you tomorrow evening,' she said as she walked away.

'But . . .' Charles Paris cursed inwardly. 'Yes, see you tomorrow evening.'

He slouched disconsolately towards his digs, in the opposite direction from Geraldine Romelle. And back to his bottle of Bell's.

FOURTEEN

I t was the ping announcing the arrival of a text that woke him the next morning. Before seven o'clock, which he reckoned was a bit early for a working actor (not to mention a drinking one).

Because he didn't send many texts he didn't receive many either. The one that had just arrived could only be from the *Hamlet* stage management or from Peri Maitland. It was the latter.

'GIVE ME AN ADDRESS FROM WHICH I CAN ARRANGE A CAR TO PICK YOU UP AT ELEVEN THIRTY. PERI.'

The vehicle which arrived five minutes early at Charles's digs very nearly qualified as a limousine. It was a private hire car, driven by a uniformed chauffeur who gave the impression that he would talk or not according to the wishes of his passenger. Charles didn't feel like any chit-chat, so they drove in silence out of Marlborough in the direction of Frome. But before they reached the town, the car veered off along a network of country lanes till it turned through the tall gates of what a discreet sign announced to be a 'boutique hotel'. The chauffeur parked in front of the main door of a perfectly proportioned Georgian mansion.

His passenger couldn't help but be impressed. This was presumably how a public relations agency ferried its celebrity clients around the country. Didn't they realize that he was only Charles Paris, jobbing actor? A minicab would have been quite sufficient.

The chauffeur ushered him into a reception area almost exactly like the hallway set of a television play in which Charles had played a young member of an Edwardian family about to be decimated by the First World War. ('Charles Paris showed about as much backbone as an overboiled piece of macaroni.' – *The Spectator*.)

There he was met by a young woman with a black trouser suit and a Russian accent. As the chauffeur receded (presumably to pick up some superstar from an airport), she led Charles through a corridor to a door, on which she tapped. Granted admission, she opened the door, ushered him in and said, 'Your guest, Mr Driscoll.'

That was a surprise to Charles. It had never occurred to him that Peri Maitland wouldn't be on her own. She was there, of course, dressed in another perfect suit and inhumanly perfect make-up, sitting at a low table on which stood a silver tray bearing a silver coffee pot and bone china cups. The man who rose to greet their guest was around fifty, gym-toned, grey hair worn slightly long but beautifully cut. He wore a tailored black suit with a subtle gridwork of blue lines in the weave and a pink shirt open at the neck. Had Charles Paris, in one of his occasional forays into directing, been casting the part of a PR consultant, he would have rejected the guy as too obvious.

'Good morning.' The man gave an unfeasibly firm handshake. 'I'm Dan.'

'Charles Paris.'

'Peri you know obviously.' The man gestured to a chair. 'Would you care for some coffee?'

Charles said he would and the man poured it himself, far too modern to let the task be performed by the woman in the room. As he passed the cup across, he said, 'I'm a director of Pridmore Baines. Though I say it myself, we are one of the most successful public relations companies in the country. In fact, I don't like the term "public relations", it's outdated. I'm sure Peri would agree with me when I say what we do these days is more crisis management, reputation management and damage limitation.' He smiled a professional smile, leaving it open as to whether what he'd just said was a joke or not. Charles thought it probably wasn't.

'And obviously the situation around the Tony Copeland production of *Hamlet* has given us a few headaches. Events like the accidents to Jared Root and Katrina Selsey . . . well, let's just say the management of publicity surrounding them requires very careful handling.'

It all sounded a bit clinical to Charles, but when he thought about it – which he hadn't much before – he supposed that 'management of publicity' was exactly what public relations companies did.

He noticed an anxious look flashed from Peri to her boss. In spite of Dan Driscoll's slick routine, she still looked nervous and Charles had to remind himself that she had a lot to be nervous about. He was in danger of letting himself be intimidated by their presentation skills, whereas in fact he had the upper hand. He possessed the important information that Peri Maitland had lied to the police. It was time he said something.

'Listen, Dan, I don't know if you know why I contacted Peri.'

'Of course I do. As my employee, she has told me everything.'

'Well, look, I'm kind of intrigued by Katrina Selsey's death.'

'You and the entire country.'

'Yes, but I'm even more intrigued because I was the person who found her body.'

Dan Driscoll communicated annoyance to his junior. 'Peri didn't tell me that.'

'Well, I did find it,' Charles went on. 'So needless to say, I've talked to the police about that. They talked to Peri, who told them she was on a train to London before that evening's performance started. And yet she was seen that same evening at the Grand Theatre helping Katrina Selsey transfer her belongings into the star dressing room.'

'Who saw me?' asked Peri, speaking for the first time.

'I don't think that's relevant at the moment,' said Charles, 'but I know it's true. So there's one simple question that I want answering. Why did you lie to the Detective Constable Whittam, Peri?'

The girl looked instantly across to her boss. She had brought him there for a reason, which was presumably to answer the kind of difficult questions Charles had just asked.

Dan Driscoll smiled the professional smile of the conciliator, and Peri Maitland looked relieved. Charles could see they were quite a team, the two of them. They worked together seamlessly, and he reckoned they had got themselves out of far trickier diplomatic challenges than the one they currently faced.

'Listen, Charles,' said Dan. 'Peri made a mistake. She's big enough to admit that. We've all made mistakes. I'm sure you've made mistakes in your life.'

Where shall I start? thought Charles.

'So what we all have to ask ourselves,' Dan Driscoll continued silkily, 'is how much harm Peri's mistake has caused. And would greater harm be caused by her admitting the mistake more publicly than just to us, or might it be better to leave things as they are?'

'If it turns out that Katrina Selsey was murdered,' said Charles, 'then I don't think "leaving things as they are" is really an option.'

The PR consultant winced, as if Charles had committed some terrible social *faux pas*. 'Now I don't believe anyone's mentioned the word "murder". I think you're being a little overdramatic there.' A patronizing smile. 'A habit to which people in your profession are sometimes prone.'

The old 'luvvie' accusation again. 'Look, I—'

'Let me continue, Charles. Peri was questioned on the telephone by this Detective Constable Whittam. It was a moment of stress for her. She had only recently heard about Katrina Selsey's death and suddenly she's being asked questions on the lines of –' he dropped into the voice of a standard blundering copper – '"Where were you on the night of the fourteenth?" . . . Like she was some kind of suspect. Peri knew she'd done nothing wrong and she thought, as many of us might, that rather than getting involved in a no doubt time-consuming police enquiry, one small white lie would let her off the hook. So she told Detective Constable Whittam that she had caught an earlier train to London than the one she actually had. End of story.'

He was good, Charles had to admit. The sweet reasonableness with which Dan had put Peri's case made arguing against it seem almost churlish. But sometimes one just had to be a bit churlish.

'Listen,' Charles began, 'the police are investigating Katrina Selsey's death. They're not going to get very far in that process if everybody withholds information from them.' Which was, when he thought about it, a bit rich from someone who'd failed to report what Dennis Demetriades had told him.

'Charles, I can see your point,' said Dan, 'and I would be in complete agreement with you, but for the fact—' He was interrupted by his mobile ringing. He checked the display and said, 'Sorry, I must take this. About Elton,' he mouthed to Peri Maitland. Putting the phone to his ear and moving to the door, he said, 'Dan Pridmore. Listen, I gather there's been a problem, which I'm sure we can sort out without too much aggravation on . . .' The door closed behind him.

Charles Paris and Peri Maitland looked at each other. She didn't seem inclined to talk, and he didn't think he'd get much out of her until her boss was back in the room. She had become almost like another of the agency's celebrity clients, who'd stepped over the mark, but whose gaffes and misdemeanours Dan could finesse away by 'management of publicity'.

'Would you like some more coffee?' asked Peri, the perfect hostess.

Charles said he would, but what was in the pot had gone cold, so she rang for the hotel staff. The Russian girl reappeared. Peri gave the order and, taking the tray, the Russian girl left, saying, 'Yes, of course, Mrs Driscoll.'

And suddenly Charles Paris understood. But he didn't say anything. Not right then. Nor indeed when Peri's boss reappeared, full of smooth apology. He'd let the conversation run a little longer.

'Anyway,' said Dan, 'we were just arguing – no, that's too strong a word. We were just discussing whether the police need ever know about Peri's slight finessing of the truth.'

'I would say that rather depends on how much she knows.'

'What do you mean, Charles?'

'Well, say she actually witnessed Katrina Selsey's death, then the information she has does become rather important, doesn't it?'

Charles watched the girl as he said this. Hard to read through her armour of make-up, but he reckoned his words had upset her. Peri opened her mouth to speak, but Dan intervened before she could say anything.

'Of course she didn't witness the death. If she'd done that she would have informed the police immediately. Isn't that right, Peri?'

'Well . . .' But she was only momentarily undecided. 'Yes, of course I would.'

'Listen, Charles,' said Dan, all avuncular now, 'I spoke of public relations as being at times "damage limitation", but a lot of it is also "conflict resolution", and conflicts only arise when the people or groups of people involved have different agendas. So I want to know what your agenda is, Charles.'

'How do you mean?'

'What are you hoping to get out of this morning's meeting? And please don't say something pious and meaningless like "the truth".'

'I wasn't about to.'

'Good. I mean, is it money you're after?'

Charles was shocked. 'What, you think I'm trying to black-mail you for my silence?'

'It wouldn't be the first time that kind of thing had happened.'

'It'd be a first for me.' He was still shaken by the sugges-tion he might have been after money. Interesting that the possibility had been raised, though. And it confirmed the direc-tion in which his mind was moving. 'Dan, there's a question I'd like to ask you . . .'

The man spread his hands wide, all bluff honesty. 'Ask away.'

'Why are you in this hotel under false names?'

That shook him, but only briefly. The bland exterior was restored as Dan replied, 'It's something we do quite a lot in our business. Many of our clients, as you know, are very high profile. So they are frequently booked into hotels under false names. And though Peri and I don't claim that kind of fame for ourselves, tabloid journalists know our client list and might read something into our booking into a hotel under our own names.'

'That "something" being the fact that one of your high-profile clients is also booked in under a false name?'

'I couldn't possibly comment,' came the well-oiled reply.

'Well,' said Charles, deciding finally that the time had come to take charge, 'that explanation might convince some people, but I'm afraid I don't buy it.'

'Oh?'

'I'm a simple soul. I don't look for more complicated explanations when there's an obvious one. Your real names are Dan Pridmore and Peri Maitland, and yet you're booked in here under the names of "Mr and Mrs Driscoll".'

'Yes, it seemed a harmless name to choose and—'

'The obvious – indeed the traditional – reason for two unmarried people booking into a hotel as "Mr and Mrs" is because they're having an affair.'

Charles Paris knew from the expressions on their faces that he'd got it right. So, taking advantage of the moment of shock, he went on, 'And I think that's why you don't want the police investigating Peri's movements, why she lied about catching a train back to London when in fact she was coming to join you here. You're just afraid the details of your affair will somehow get back to your wife.'

Dan Pridmore's silence was eloquent. He was caught in that oldest and most predictable of scenarios – the boss having it off with his junior from the office.

'So . . . you asked about my agenda . . . I'm not after money. Nor do I have any kind of idealistic notion that "the truth should always out". I'm quite happy to agree not to mention anything about Peri's lies to the police.' His listeners looked relieved at that, but still wary. 'However,' Charles went on, 'my agenda – what I want out of the deal – is that Peri tells me exactly what happened that evening with Katrina Selsey in the Grand Theatre. She tells me that and, so far as I'm concerned, the matter is closed.'

'Well, I'm sure Peri will be more than happy to—'

Charles cut Dan Pridmore off. 'My other condition is that she tells me one to one – without you in the room.'

The public relations guru looked across at his mistress. She gave a curt nod and he left.

Peri Maitland stared defiantly at Charles, challenging him to interrogate her. So, if that was the role she had cast him in, it was a role he was happy to play.

'All right, Peri, let's go back to the night Katrina died . . .'
No response. 'Presumably it was her idea to make the move
into the star dressing room?'

'Are you asking if *I* suggested it?' She was very affronted.

'No, just checking facts. I remember her saying at
rehearsal that she ought to be in there . . . on that occasion
when she endearingly described the rest of the company as
"nonentities".'

'Katrina was very immature, just a spoilt child, really.'

'Did you like her, Peri?'

The girl shrugged. 'She was a client. Whether I actually
liked her or not wasn't relevant.'

'And as a Personal Manager, it was your job to put up with
her tantrums and see to it that she always got her own way.'

'Up to a point, yes. It was very early days in our professional relationship. We hadn't worked together for much more
than a month.'

'No. I was just thinking a few days back . . .'

'Hm?'

'When Tony Copeland summoned us all in at nine thirty
and then bawled Katrina out for Twittering or whatever it is
you call it.'

'I remember.'

'Well, I was passing the Green Room on my way in that
morning . . . and I heard you and Katrina having the most
almighty row.'

'So?'

'She was being very demanding, saying that you should
concentrate on her rather than your other clients.'

'As I said, she was very immature. Constantly throwing her
toys out of the pram. Anyway, why's that relevant, Charles?'

'Well, look, Katrina Selsey's was a suspicious death. Under
which circumstances . . . it seems reasonable to wonder who
might have anything against her.'

Peri Maitland's thickly-eyelashed eyes widened. 'Charles,
for God's sake! You're not suggesting I murdered Katrina, are
you?'

'No. I'm just reviewing possibilities. Making a mental list
of people who might have had something against her.'

'Could be a long list, Charles.'

'Maybe. She did seem to have the knack of putting people's backs up.'

'But it's also a rather pointless mental list for you to be making.'

'Why?'

'Because Katrina wasn't murdered.'

'You know that for a fact?'

'Yes. Her death was accidental.'

'Perhaps you could tell me what makes you so sure of that, Peri . . .?'

'Tell you my exact movements the night she died?' she asked with a wry smile.

'That would be very nice, yes.'

'Very well. I had told everyone in the *Hamlet* company that I was going to get a cab to Swindon and catch the train for London. And I left the theatre in time to do just that.'

'Before the performance started?'

'Yes.'

'Though, of course, you had no intention of going back to London. You were going to come here to join Dan.'

'You do make it sound rather squalid, Charles.' He didn't say anything. She'd used the word; he hadn't.

'Anyway, I'm about halfway here in a cab when I get a text from Katrina. She says something really important's come up and she needs me back at the theatre immediately.' Peri sighed. 'The temptation to pretend I hadn't got the text was huge. And what Katrina regarded as "something really important" could be something really trivial. But looking after her was my job, so I got the cab to turn round and back to the theatre I went. The Stage Doorkeeper fortunately wasn't in his cubbyhole, so no one saw me arrive.'

She sighed again. 'And, needless to say, it wasn't anything important. Just Katrina's fatuous plan to move her belongings into the star dressing room while Sam Newton-Reid was busy onstage. Well, I'd by then realized that it was often simpler just to go along with what Katrina wanted than to make an issue of it. So I said I'd help her with the stuff, intending to come straight back here and leave her to face the consequences of her selfishness. I cannot imagine that what she'd done would have got much sympathy from the *Hamlet* company.'

'That is an understatement.' Charles Paris looked Peri Maitland steadily in the eye. 'So what happened?'

Another sigh, but this one was different. The previous ones had been reactions to Katrina Selsey's solipsistic behaviour. There was more pain this time. It wasn't easy for Peri to re-create the scene.

'OK, so we shift Katrina's stuff into the star dressing room. And we move poor old Sam Newton-Reid's stuff into the dressing room she's vacating.'

'Does anyone see you doing this?'

'I don't think so. I didn't see anyone. Everyone was either onstage or in the wings.'

Charles decided to keep quiet about what he'd heard from Dennis Demetriades as, becoming increasingly tense, Peri Maitland went on, 'OK, the deed was done, my duty had been discharged and I was on my way out of there. But just before I left the dressing room, Katrina said she was going to repair her make-up.'

She was silent for a moment, marshalling her memories. 'She picked up her mascara from the table, opened it and brought the brush up to her lashes . . .

'Then I'm not exactly clear what happened. It was like the mascara stung her eye or . . . I don't know. She kind of leapt up from her seat in shock and fell backwards over it. And the back of her head went down hard on the stone floor.' Peri Maitland winced. 'I can still hear the sound it made. I can't believe how loud it was. I sometimes wake in the night hearing it.

'I could see immediately that Katrina was dead. So I just got the hell out of the place.'

FIFTEEN

What Peri had told him completely changed all of Charles's thinking about Katrina Selsey's death. It had been an accident. And yet not totally an accident. He remembered seeing the discoloration around the dead girl's eye, as if she had rubbed it. And the only witness of her actual death had talked about Katrina's eye being stung. What was in the mascara? Had it been sabotaged?

Of course, he'd asked Peri these questions, but she couldn't help. She hadn't inspected the dressing room, just got out of the Grand Theatre as quickly as possible, hoping that no one would ever know that she had returned there at all that evening. She had got a cab to the hotel and joined up with her married lover.

Not for the first time Charles Paris felt the frustration of the amateur detective. He bet the police had done forensic tests and already knew what noxious substance had been introduced into that mascara tube. They were probably well on their way to knowing who put it there too. How could he compete when the police had all the evidence and information? It wasn't fair.

Idly, Charles wondered whether, assuming Peri Maitland had been telling the truth about Katrina Selsey's last moments, the death could be regarded as murder. If, as seemed likely, the mascara tube had been doctored by someone with a grudge against the girl, would he or she be legally responsible for the death? It was reaction to the pain in her eye which had made Katrina leap back, stumble over her chair and have her fatal fall. But the mascara-adulterator couldn't have anticipated that sequence of events. And didn't the definition of 'murder' involve the concept of intent? Charles wished he knew more about the law, but he reckoned the most the perpetrator could be charged with would be manslaughter.

It was still a very vindictive thing to do. Depending on what was actually in the mascara tube, it could have caused permanent

damage to the girl's eye. And though Katrina Selsey had gone
out of her way to antagonize many of the *Hamlet* company,
who would feel strongly enough to take that kind of revenge?

These thoughts circled around Charles Paris's mind as the
private hire car drove him back from the boutique hotel. The
chauffeur hadn't gone off to collect a superstar from an airport,
he had just waited for Charles. He was set to take him back
to his digs, but Charles, realizing he hadn't had any lunch,
asked to be dropped at The Pessimist's Arms instead. He'd
got *The Times* with him; he wouldn't look lonely if he was
doing the crossword.

He ordered a pint and, remembering his unfortunate experience of the Sunday Roast, asked for a ham sandwich. Surely
not even The Pessimist's Arms could get a ham sandwich wrong?

Charles was about to take his pint and paper to the alcove
he'd occupied before when he saw someone he recognized.
Milly Henryson, with a glass of sparkling mineral water and
a noxiously unappetizing wrap on a plate in front of her. She
looked very forlorn.

'Hi.' Charles acknowledged her and then felt uncertain as
to whether he should force his company on her. Fortunately,
she gestured to the empty chair opposite and said, 'If you'd
like to join me . . .?'

He sat down and grinned. 'I'm rather surprised that this is
your sort of place.'

'It isn't,' she said ruefully. 'You are witnessing my first and
– having just tasted that wrap – very definitely my last visit.
No, I was just at a loose end and . . .'

Oh dear. She did look rather upset. Charles hoped nothing
had gone wrong between her and Sam Newton-Reid. He bit
back the urge to ask a how's-lover-boy type of question.

But she answered without its being asked. And the news
was not terminal.

'Sam's at an interview in London. For a leading part in a
new drama series the Beeb are doing.' She couldn't keep the
wistfulness out of her voice. However much love is felt for
the person who's got lucky, there's an instinctive bit of every
actor which wishes they'd got the break instead.

'He'll be back in time for the show tonight?'

'Oh. Of course he will. It's all been organized by Tony Copeland, whose television company is involved in the series somehow. He's got fingers in so many pies.'

'You can say that again.'

'And now Tony's backing Sam in *Hamlet*, he's going to get him lots of other stuff to "raise his profile".'

'Seems to be the way things are done these days,' said Charles Paris lugubriously, wondering whether he'd ever actually had a 'profile'. 'There are actors who—'

He was interrupted by the sullen barman bringing his food across. Looking at the curling bread, garishly pink filling and sad garnish of crisps, Charles realized that he'd been wrong. The Pessimist's Arms could even get a ham sandwich wrong.

He took a bite to see whether the presentation was outclassed by the taste. It wasn't.

'So . . .' said Milly Henryson in a tone close to despair, 'I wonder how much longer Sam and I will be acting in the same kind of shows.'

'Oh, you'll get the breaks. You're very good too.'

The look the girl gave him showed that his words had not carried sufficient conviction. Milly was a realist. She wasn't 'very good'. She was 'quite good', and she knew it. She could have a perfectly satisfactory career in the theatre – particularly given how pretty she was – but she was never going to be in the same league as her boyfriend. Or perhaps, Charles thought gloomily, her current boyfriend.

'And I don't even feel secure that I'm going to keep the part of Ophelia.'

'How do you mean?'

'Well, I've been told I'm playing it, right, but I'm still expected to do some of the stuff I was doing as an ASM. You know, I've been told I've got to help with the get-out on Saturday night.'

Charles was surprised by this news, but he tried to sound reassuring as he said, 'I'm sure that's just a temporary thing. You know, with everything else that's been going on, the stage management haven't yet had time to bring in someone else. I'm absolutely certain Tony Copeland is planning to keep you on as Ophelia.'

'Oh yes? You don't think he's more likely to get in a "name" for the West End? Someone who brings a bit more publicity with them? One of the *StarHunt* runners-up, maybe?'

'I'm sure that's not the sort of thing that Tony'd do.' Though even as he said the words Charles knew it was exactly the sort of thing Tony'd do. He tried to shift the direction of the conversation. 'Did Sam go up to London by taking a cab to Swindon and then getting the train?'

'Oh no, he got the full Tony Copeland Productions treatment.'

'Meaning?'

'He was driven up and he's being driven back by Doug Haye.'

'There's posh for you. He's very honoured. I'm never quite sure what Doug does in Tony's set-up.'

'More or less everything, it seems. Being Tony's driver is his main job, I think, but he helps out with other stuff.'

Milly spoke distractedly, though. The desolation Charles had seen in her face when she thought she was alone had returned.

'It'll be all right,' he said. 'Sam adores you.'

'Yes, he does now,' she agreed. 'But if his career takes off stratospherically . . .'

'No reason why he shouldn't continue to adore you. He seems to me an extremely sensible young man. Head very definitely screwed on the right way.'

'I hope so. I just couldn't manage without him. And I know having relationships with actors is difficult.'

'How do you know?' asked Charles, trying to lighten the mood. 'Have you had a lot of them?'

'No. But when I said I wanted to go into the business, my headmistress at school always said that being married to an actor was sheer hell.'

'Oh.' Then Charles realized that she was talking about his wife, Frances. Which didn't make Milly's remark the most comforting he had ever heard.

After the couple of pints at lunch he had gone back and fallen asleep. When he woke, his digs still didn't seem very congenial, so he went to the theatre early to have another go at *The Times* crossword in the Green Room. The grid didn't prove very tractable. He was having one of those days when the clues seemed blankly impenetrable. His conversations with Peri Maitland and Milly Henryson had lowered his mood and his cruciverbal incompetence did nothing to lift it.

The Green Room door was open and Charles heard footsteps approaching from the Stage Door. And voices. 'Thank you very much,' Sam Newton-Reid was saying. 'It would have been a hell of a trek to do it by train.'

'No problem. I had stuff to sort out in London too.'

Charles Paris recognized the second voice immediately. He had last heard it in discussion with Bazza at The Pessimist's Arms. Moving quickly to the Green Room door, Charles was quick enough to see Sam Newton-Reid turning out of sight on the stairs up to his dressing room.

And to see the stockily-built figure making his way out of the Stage Door.

It was Tony Copeland's factotum, Doug Haye.

SIXTEEN

A shrewd observer might have noticed a slightly distracted quality in the performances of the Ghost of Hamlet's Father and First Gravedigger in that night's *Hamlet*. Charles Paris's mind was full and racing. He recalled every detail of the conversation he'd overheard in The Pessimist's Arms after Jared Root's accident. At the time he remembered thinking it could have implied that Bazza had set up the sabotage. Now Charles knew that the stagehand had been talking to Doug Haye, a whole new set of possibilities opened up.

He'd never seen Bazza joining the post-show drinkers in the pub nearest to the Grand Theatre, but then the man was a local who lived in Marlborough and probably had his own favourite drinking hole. On the premise that he had once seen the stagehand there, Charles reckoned it might be The Pessimist's Arms. So he found his weary footsteps wending towards the same unattractive venue for the second time that day.

His hunch had been right. Bazza was sitting in the same alcove as he had with Doug Haye, but now in lugubrious isolation. He was more than halfway down a pint, which gave Charles the perfect opening. 'Can I get you another of those?'

The lanky young man looked up with something that could almost have been a grin. 'Never been known to refuse an offer like that.'

'What is it?'

'Six-X.'

'Leave it with me.' At the bar, reckoning that Bazza as a local would know the best beer, Charles ordered two pints of Wadworth's 6X and returned to the alcove with them. He took an exploratory swig. 'Excellent.'

'Never fails,' Bazza agreed. 'This may be a pretty grotty pub, but they know how to look after their beer.'

This masculine badinage was all very well, but Charles

realized that he hadn't really prepared for the conversation he was about to embark on. He'd been so preoccupied with the connection he'd now made between Bazza and Doug Haye that he hadn't worked out how to broach a subject which might very quickly lead to accusations.

Still, having got to this point, he had to lumber in somehow. 'I actually wanted to talk to you, Bazza,' he began clumsily, 'about Doug Haye.'

'Tony Copeland's Rottweiler? Why?'

'It goes back to the accident that happened to Jared Root . . .'

'Oh yes?' There was a new caution in the young man's eyes.

Charles was circumspect. He didn't want to leap straight to a confession of his eavesdropping. 'Well, given what happened there . . . and given what's happened since with Katrina . . . there's been a lot of gossip backstage.'

'When isn't there a lot of gossip backstage? You should know what theatre people are like by now.'

'Yes, of course.'

'So are you saying you've been listening to backstage gossip, Charles?'

'Well . . .'

'About what in particular? Some illicit shagging been going on? I'm usually fairly quick to spot that, but I haven't been aware of much going on with the *Hamlet* lot . . . though there might be something developing between Rosencrantz and Guildenstern. If you know about that . . . Come on, Charles, give me the dirt.'

'Sorry, I can't. Quite possible there has been something going on, but I haven't been aware of it either. Anyway, that wasn't what I wanted to talk to you about.'

'Oh?'

Charles was not finding this easy. 'The fact is, Bazza, as you say, actors are very good at spreading rumours around, and getting the wrong end of sticks, and building up conspiracy theories.' The stagehand didn't say anything, just looked at him as he struggled on. 'And obviously there's been a lot of talk about the two . . . accidents . . . and whether or not they're connected.'

'So what makes you think they might be?'

'I didn't actually say I thought that. I just said that a lot of people in the company do think that.'

'OK, so the show's got some jinx on it, is that it? It is *Hamlet* we're doing, Charles, not *Macbeth*.'

Time to stop beating about the bush. 'Some people have been saying that the accident to Jared was arranged.'

'Arranged? How do you mean – arranged?'

'That it was set up. That the piece of the skull was made to fall on him deliberately.'

Bazza's eyes were very narrow now. 'And who would want to do that?'

'Or then again, to ask another pertinent question, who would have the opportunity to do that?'

'What're you saying, Charles?'

'I'm saying that, if Jared's injury wasn't accidental, then the only people who could have set it up would be members of the backstage crew.'

'Like me, for instance?'

'If you like.'

'I don't like at all. I don't like being accused of things by overdramatizing actors.'

'I'm not accusing you.' .

'Well, you're coming damned close to it. Too close for my liking.'

'But if it wasn't an accident—'

'Do you have any proof, Charles?'

'Not proof as such.'

'Of course you don't. Because there is no proof. A piece of scenery fell by accident on Jared Root – that's all that happened. Anyway, why do you imagine that I – or any other member of the backstage crew – might want to sabotage the show we're working on?'

'I can only think of one reason why you might do that.'

'And what is it?'

'Because you were paid to do so.'

Bazza reacted as if he'd been slapped in the face. 'Oh, I see. And who are you suggesting might have paid me?'

'Doug Haye,' Charles Paris replied coolly.

That brought Bazza to his feet, towering over his accuser. For a moment Charles feared that he was going to be hit, but the stagehand restrained himself. Instead, in a hissing whisper he spat out, 'Don't you ever dare spread that accusation anywhere! If you do, by God you'll regret it!'

And with that Bazza stormed out of The Pessimist's Arms, leaving his second pint of 6X untouched.

Charles Paris sipped away at his own, feeling quite pleased with himself. Though the stagehand hadn't actually admitted to accepting money from Doug Haye to arrange Jared's accident, the strength of his reaction demonstrated that Charles was very definitely on the right track.

It seemed silly not to drink Bazza's pint as well as his own, so Charles felt suitably mellow when time was called and he left The Pessimist's Arms. A nightcap of Bell's back at the digs and he thought he'd sleep well.

The weather had changed. He must remember to take an overcoat with him when he went to the theatre the following day. The autumn days were still mild, but the evenings had started to get chilly.

He'd done the route from pub to digs so often that he didn't have to think about it. Left out of The Pessimist's Arms, along the road, another left, through an alley, turn right. Less than ten minutes.

It was when he was in the alley that he heard the footsteps behind him. Close behind him. He quickened his pace. But when he heard his name called, he stopped and turned. To find himself facing the solid bulk of Doug Haye.

The force with which the man's left hand grabbed his lapels slammed Charles Paris against the wall. On Doug Haye's upraised hand the inadequate light from a distant street-lamp glinted on the metal edge of a knuckleduster.

SEVENTEEN

'**H**old it there, Doug!' said a voice. And Doug did hold it there. To the considerable relief of Charles Paris. The knuckleduster had stopped millimetres away from his chin.

'Let go of him.'

The grip on Charles's lapels was released with some reluctance. He looked towards the silhouette framed by the entrance to the alleyway.

'I think we ought to talk,' said Tony Copeland.

The producer wasn't staying in a lavish boutique hotel like the people from Pridmore Baines. He had opted for an old coaching inn in the centre of town, solid, unexciting. As well as a bedroom, he had a sitting room, though, and it was there that he had the bottle of room-service whisky delivered, along with an ice bucket and a single glass.

'I don't drink,' he said, 'but I gather you do.'

'Well . . .' Charles shrugged sheepishly. 'Has been known.'

'Help yourself.'

Charles did so.

'I'm not going to apologize for Doug's actions because that might suggest that I had something to do with them, that he was acting on my instructions. He's very loyal and he makes decisions very much off his own bat . . . both of which are qualities which I admire in people who work for me.'

Tony Copeland was unruffled; there was little intonation in his voice. Off-screen he was totally unlike the waspish critic of *StarHunt*. Once again he wore his uniform of pinstriped suit, tie and rimless glasses, looking more than ever like an accountant. And accountancy, the management and manipulation of money, was, of course, a large part of his job as a theatre producer. Whether arranging accidents to befall his stars was another part of the job description Charles Paris could only, for the time being, conjecture.

The one thing he did know for sure was that Tony Copeland had an agenda. He hadn't invited a minor actor from his production of *Hamlet* into his room and supplied him with a bottle of whisky purely out of the goodness of his heart.

'All right,' said Charles. 'I can understand why you don't want to admit responsibility for Doug's actions, but do you at least know why he attacked me?'

'He attacked you,' came the cool reply, 'because he didn't want you spreading rumours in the company about Jared Root's accident.'

'Like the rumour that it wasn't an accident?'

'Maybe.' The producer shrugged.

'You don't seem that bothered.'

'I'm not. I have too many important responsibilities to worry about backstage gossip.'

'And what if it were more than gossip?'

'What do you mean, Charles?'

'I'm pretty sure Jared's injuries were caused deliberately.'

'Oh? And what do you base that on?'

So Charles related to him the conversation he'd overheard between Doug Haye and Bazza in The Pessimist's Arms.

At the end of his account Tony Copeland looked singularly underwhelmed. 'There's more than one interpretation to what you heard.'

'Oh, come on.'

'And even if it's true, that Doug did pay Bazza to cause the accident, the charge would never stand up in a court of law.'

'Maybe not, but from the way Bazza reacted when I talked about it this evening, I know it is true.'

That merited no more than another shrug. 'And what would Doug's motive have been in taking that rather extreme step of causing an injury to Jared Root?'

'Look, Tony, it was clear to everyone in the company that Jared, however popular he may be as a singer, couldn't act to save his life. With him playing the part, it really was "*Hamlet* without the Prince".'

'The box office advance was very good, just on the strength of his name.'

'Yes, but once people started seeing the show, once the reviews came out—'

'The age group who're interested in Jared Root don't read reviews.'

'It doesn't change my point. Word of mouth would have got around. So long as Jared stayed in the title role, this *Hamlet* was dead in the water.'

'And Doug worked all this out for himself, did he? And out of the goodness of his heart he made arrangements with Bazza to solve the production's central problem?'

'I'm not suggesting Doug worked it out for himself. I'm suggesting he was following instructions.'

'Really?' Still not a flutter in the producer's calm demeanour.

'I'm suggesting that Jared had served his purpose. Once he'd generated far more publicity than you're ever going to get for your average production of *Hamlet*, he was surplus to requirements. But obviously this play of all plays needs someone bloody good in the name part. You'd seen Sam Newton-Reid give a stunning performance in a pub theatre in Battersea. You saw a way of getting even more publicity, as well as a Hamlet who could turn the production into a very good one. And you saw in Sam a talent that you could nurture.'

'I see, so it's me now? Not Doug acting off his own bat, but me giving him instructions?'

'Yes.'

'Hm. You do have a vivid imagination, Charles.' Tony Copeland's words were insufferably patronizing. 'Not to mention a lack of inhibition about accusing me of deliberately injuring a member of my company.'

Charles Paris looked straight into the producer's cold blue eyes. 'I'm convinced that's what happened, Tony.'

The eye contact was held. Charles was the first to turn away.

'Well,' said Tony Copeland, 'suppose you were right . . .? Suppose I did engineer this rather complicated crime you're accusing me of? What would you do about it?'

'Well, I—'

'I would remind you, of course, that the management of the

Grand Theatre have conducted a full enquiry into what happened. The insurance assessors have checked the place out too. No evidence of foul play was found.'

'Bazza would know how to cover his tracks.'

'Whether or not he had tracks to cover I have no idea. I go back to my previous question, Charles. If your conjecture did turn out to be true, what would you do about it?'

'Well . . .' He wasn't quite sure of the next step. Having got Tony Copeland virtually to admit involvement in the crime, he must find a way of capitalizing on the moment. 'I could go to the police,' he said defiantly.

'Ooh yes, they'd really love to hear the theories of a precious luvvie of an actor, wouldn't they?'

Tony was right. There had been previous occasions when Charles had tried to convince the police of someone's wrongdoing, and his treatment had never been less than patronizing.

'Quite honestly,' the producer resumed, 'you can do what you like. It won't get you anywhere. You go to the police, they'll laugh you out of court. And talking of courts, if your accusation ever got that far – which it wouldn't – you'd be blown away there too, Charles. You have no idea of the quality of lawyers that Tony Copeland Productions can afford.'

Charles knew he was losing ground and made one more desperate sally. 'Suppose I went to court about Doug Haye's attacking me in the alley?'

The producer smiled blandly. 'Did Doug Haye attack you in an alley?'

'Yes, of course he did. With a knuckleduster.'

'Ah, well, if he used a knuckleduster, no doubt you have some dramatic bruising to show for it?'

'As you know, you stopped him before he actually hit me.'

'Did I? I don't recall.'

'You were a witness.'

'Yes, I was a witness, and I don't recall seeing anything untoward. You and Doug were having a chat in the alleyway. I joined you, then you came back to my room for a drink . . . Do top your glass up, by the way, Charles.' Another bland smile as Charles couldn't resist doing as he was told. 'And that is my recollection of what happened between us this evening.'

'I see. And when I walk out of this hotel am I likely to be attacked again by Doug Haye?'

'What's this "again"? You haven't been attacked by him once.'

Charles was getting frustrated by all this blandness. 'So you're saying I'm not at risk from Doug Haye?'

'Of course not.'

'You've called off the Rottweiler, have you?'

'What a very strange expression to use in describing one of my most trusted employees.'

There was only one ploy left to get a reaction out of the man. 'Of course,' Charles announced, 'what happened to Jared Root would be relatively unimportant if it wasn't connected to what happened to Katrina Selsey.'

The eyelids flickered twice behind the rimless glasses. By Tony Copeland's standards, that was a big reaction. 'Do you know that the two incidents are connected?' he asked.

'It would be strange if they weren't.'

'What do you mean? Do you know something?' Clearly, these questions mattered more than anything else Tony Copeland had asked that evening.

'Well, look at the similarities. Both of the victims were inexperienced actors who'd come into this production by winning television talent shows. Both have been replaced by better actors.'

'You think Milly Henryson is better than Katrina Selsey?' asked the producer sharply.

'She's certainly more experienced. She has a more natural way of dealing with Shakespeare's language.'

Tony nodded, then looked a little wistful. 'I thought Katrina was a genuine talent. Yes, inexperienced – and she had a lot to learn about backstage manners – but I think she could have gone a long way.' He stopped for a moment as a new thought came to him. 'Charles when you say the accidents are connected . . . and you've just accused me of deliberately sabotaging Jared Root . . . are you putting me in the frame for the accident to Katrina Selsey as well?'

Time to brazen it out, thought Charles as he said, 'Yes.'

'Oh,' said the producer with the hint of a smile. 'Nice to know what my employees think of me.'

'The two must be connected. There are too many coincidences for them not to be.'

'I can see the way your mind's working, Charles, but you're completely wrong.' Tony Copeland tapped his chin hard as he pieced his thoughts together. 'Jared Root was a problem. As rehearsals went on it was clear he was never going to reach the standard required . . . so either I would have had to pull the plug on the show . . . or something had to be done there.'

He spoke pragmatically, virtually admitting the crime, but with no anxiety. He knew Charles had no power to get him convicted.

'And I saw ways that I could use Jared's accident to my advantage from the publicity point of view. Tweeting bulletins about his injuries and his recovery, I could keep the interest running for a long time.'

'So it was you who sent out all the tweets on Jared's behalf?'

'Of course,' said Tony Copeland without emotion. 'But Katrina,' he went on, 'I had no motive to want her out of the show. Indeed, with Jared out, she was the only contact I had with the young demographic who'd followed her through *StarHunt*. With her in place and by building a bit of *A Star Is Born*-type publicity around Sam, I reckoned I could make the production profitable. So no, her death was a total body-blow to me. Last thing I wanted.' He looked straight at Charles. 'You really can remove my name from your list of suspects there.'

The actor grinned wryly. 'Of course, that's what you'd say if you had murdered her, isn't it?'

Another double eyelash-flicker registered the shock. 'Murder? Are people backstage talking about murder?' He sounded as if this genuinely was the first time he'd considered the possibility.

'You know what actors are like,' said Charles.

'Don't I just? And so who is being cast by the backstage community in the role of murderer? Is it me – or are you the only person who sees me in that light?'

'There are a lot of theories about.'

'I'm sure there are.' There was a silence. Then Tony Copeland asked, 'Do you remember a television director called Rick Landor?'

The name was foggily familiar. Oh yes, it came back to him. 'He directed some episodes of a creaky whodunnit series I was in. *Stanislas Braid*, that's right. Starring that pompous oaf Russell Bentley in the title role. I was, as I recall, a baffled village bobby, though I can't remember what I was called. Anyway, why do you ask about him?'

'He was Executive Producer on a show I was involved in some time back and I remember him talking about some unexplained deaths during the filming of that *Stanislas Braid* series.'

'Yes, there were a few.'

'And he mentioned you, Charles. Said you were particularly keen to find out what had been going on.'

'Well . . .'

'Rick even described you as a bit of an amateur sleuth.'

'Hardly.'

'You can't deny it, Charles. Seems to me you're showing more than a casual interest in Katrina Selsey's death.'

'Maybe I just—'

'I am as desperate as you are to find out exactly how that poor girl lost her life.' For the first time ever Charles heard something approaching genuine emotion in the producer's voice. 'Do let me know anything you find out.'

It was after one when he left the hotel. Tony Copeland had insisted he took the remains of the whisky bottle, which made him feel rather patronized, as if he was being given a tip.

But it had been a strange encounter, in the course of which Tony had not only virtually admitted to arranging Jared Root's exit from the production of *Hamlet*, but also appointed Charles Paris as his personal investigator into Katrina Selsey's death.

EIGHTEEN

I t had been a late night and Charles slept late the following morning. He would have slept even later, had he not been woken by his mobile ringing.

'Hello?' he said a little blearily.

'Charles?'

'Yes.'

He just had time to register the foreign accent before the caller identified himself. 'It's Tibor Pincus.'

'Good to hear you. Gosh, is this more work? Do you want me to do a single-handed re-enactment of the Battle of the Somme, playing the part of all the casualties?'

'No, I'm sorry, Charles, it's not work. It might be fun, though.'

'Oh?'

'Listen, you remember when we did the Battle of Naseby?'

'Etched on my memory. How could I ever forget?'

'And that day we were talking about Portie . . .?'

'"Portie"?'

'Yes, you remember. The actor, Portie.'

It came back. 'The one who went to the States. Made a packet over there.'

'I'm not sure how big the packet he made was. But, anyway, he's over in London at the moment and he gave me a call.'

'Right.'

'Basically, I'm meeting him for lunch at Joe Allen tomorrow and he asked if I could get "any of the old drinking crowd out" to join us . . . and I immediately thought of you, Charles.'

'Sounds like my reputation goes before me.'

'It certainly does. Well, could you make it? No doubt you're just lounging round London, resting as usual.'

'I'll have you know,' said Charles with mock-*hauteur*, 'I am currently in gainful employment.'

'Really? What's gone wrong?'

'Ha bloody ha. Nothing's gone wrong. I am currently giving my Ghost of Hamlet's Father and First Gravedigger in a Tony Copeland production of *Hamlet* at the Grand Theatre, Marlborough.'

'Oh, Lord. Is that the one where that poor kid died?'

'The very same.'

'Ah. Well, if you're down in Marlborough I suppose lunch tomorrow at Joe Allen would be out of the question.'

Charles thought about it. A boozy lunch with a couple of friends in the business was not without its appeal. And he remembered Portie as being something of a larger-than-life character. Other company members who'd made the trip up to London said it didn't take long. Cab to Swindon and the train from there to Paddington, whole journey only round an hour and a half. Quite possible to do there and back inside the day and still be in Marlborough to do an evening performance in *Hamlet*.

'By no means out of the question,' said Charles Paris.

His conversation with Tony Copeland the previous night had strengthened Charles's interest in finding out the truth about Katrina Selsey's death. He felt as if he had been given a mission by the producer to investigate on his behalf. And he trusted what Tony had said about calling off his Rottweiler Doug Haye. Nor did he anticipate any trouble from Bazza the stagehand.

So after a modest lunch (steak and ale pie, two glasses of Merlot and *The Times* crossword) at the pub he'd been to with Geraldine Romelle, it seemed natural to Charles that his steps should take him back to the Grand Theatre. The scene of the crime. He might find some clue there that had hitherto been missed, or some company member who would vouchsafe him a precious piece of information.

The Stage Doorkeeper wasn't in his cubbyhole and Charles didn't see anyone around, though distant clunking noises suggested that someone was in the stage area doing something technical – possibly brain surgery on the cranium set. So he decided to go up and have another look at the star dressing room.

He fully expected it still to be locked and sealed, as it had been since Katrina's death. But there was no sign of crime scene tape. The police must have been in that morning to open it up again, because the door gave to his hand. Which suggested that whatever investigations they had been doing were now complete. The police had reached a conclusion about how Katrina had died. Charles found it very frustrating how little likelihood there was of their ever sharing their findings with him. Maybe he'd read something about the case in a newspaper at some later date, maybe never hear any more about it.

He wondered what would happen with the star dressing room now. Surely Sam Newton-Reid would reclaim it as his rightful place? But actors are a superstitious lot. Entirely possible that the young man might feel spooked using a space that had been the scene of such a tragedy.

It was now far too tidy to be a dressing room. Everything had been scrubbed so clean that it looked as if no one had ever spread their costumes and make-up and bottles and good luck cards over its walls and tables and mirrors. Charles's optimism about finding some undiscovered clue there quickly melted away.

But actually being in the place focused his mind on his last visit. He tried to reconstruct the scene he'd encountered in the interval of *Hamlet*'s First Night. The upturned chair. Katrina Selsey lying on the stone floor, the blood pooling under her blonde hair.

And her red eye. The eye that looked as if she'd rubbed at it hard. Charles remembered Peri Maitland's words: 'It was like the mascara stung her eye.' Though he'd never used the stuff himself he'd been around enough women to know how mascara worked. There was a thin brush and a thin tube of sticky black stuff. You put the brush in the tube, then brought it out and applied it to your lashes.

But if something caustic had been introduced into the tube . . . Acid . . .? Some kind of household cleaner . . .? Bleach might do the trick. If that got on to the eyeball . . . Well, there probably wouldn't be enough of it to cause any permanent damage. But it would certainly hurt. Certainly give the receiver a nasty shock. Quite enough to make them jump backwards, fall over a chair and . . .

There were two chairs in the room. Their wooden parts

were gilded and the upholstery was crimson velveteen. Function chairs, the kind that are always stacked up in hotel basements to be brought out for dinners and weddings.

Was it possible they were the same ones that had been in the dressing room when Katrina died? Charles inspected them. On the fabric of one was a tiny pale mark. Not something stuck on, not something that had made a hole. It looked as if a drop of fluid had landed on the chair seat and leached away the colour from that tiny circle of cloth.

Charles Paris was now convinced that household bleach had been poured into the mascara tube.

Entering the Green Room to do the last few clues of *The Times* crossword – he felt confident he'd finish it today – he found Geraldine Romelle stretched out on a sofa reading her Montaigne. She was wearing those trousers midway between leggings and jeans which most women seemed to be wearing that year and they perfectly outlined her legs and thighs. The tightness of the trousers did so much of the work for him that Charles couldn't help imagining what she'd look like completely naked. Nor could he help remembering many happy afternoons he'd spent enjoying female company while on tour. And, not for the first time, by 'female company' he meant 'sex'.

They exchanged 'Hi's and he told her he'd just been upstairs. 'All the police tape's been removed from the star dressing room. It's open again.'

'Yes, I saw that.'

It struck Charles that, in his new role as Tony Copeland's investigator, he should miss no opportunity to pick company members' brains about Katrina Selsey's death, so he subtly moved the conversation in that direction. 'I had a look inside. It's like Katrina never existed.'

Geraldine shrugged, as if to say that the loss had not been a great one. 'Well,' she said, 'her absence has made for a more relaxed company.'

'And a better show.'

'Indeed. And while obviously feeling sympathy for her friends and family, I can't pretend to be sorry that she's no longer playing Ophelia.'

'Oh?' said Charles, hoping she would be encouraged to expand on this.

She was. 'I mean, I don't think I'm particularly full of myself, I haven't got that many airs and graces, but the way Katrina behaved really got up my nose.'

Another prompting, 'Oh?'

'Look, we actors are generally speaking fairly relaxed, laid-back creatures who don't stand on ceremony. But I do think youngsters starting out in the business should show a bit of respect for the greater experience of older members of the company.'

There was a slightly chippy quality in Geraldine Romelle's voice which Charles hadn't heard before. And he saw how she, playing Gertrude, and being a senior member of the company, might resent Katrina Selsey's lack of interest in her achievements in the theatre. Also, though she still looked pretty good, Geraldine was at the age when she might be worrying about her looks going. So the introduction of a disrespectful but undeniably pretty teenager into the *Hamlet* company could have antagonized her quite a bit. It might be worth investigating further what Geraldine Romelle really thought of her younger rival.

'When I looked in the star dressing room just now,' Charles began casually, 'I was trying to visualize exactly how Katrina died.'

'I'm sure everyone in the company has done that.'

'Mm.' Charles wasn't about to reveal his sources, so he went on, 'I reckon she might have had some kind of shock that made her stand up, back off and fall over her chair, then hit her head on the floor.'

'Sounds plausible.' The words were spoken lightly enough, but Charles felt sure he could hear a new tension in Geraldine's voice.

'And I wondered if, because she'd made herself so unpop-ular, someone from the company might have done something to punish her.'

'How do you mean – punish?'

'Well, Geraldine, I'm sure you've heard lots of those old actors' stories about nasty practical jokes that have been played on unpopular cast members . . .?'

'Like what?'

'Oh, like sticking pins into someone's wig or, even nastier, embedding razor blades in the old Leichner greasepaint sticks . . . you know, so that when the actor goes to make up he slashes his or her own face.'

'I've never heard of that happening,' said Geraldine tautly.

'They're probably apocryphal, but they're the kind of stories that go round after actors have had a few drinks.'

'Well, clearly I've never been involved in the right drinking sessions.'

'No.' Charles was silent for a moment before saying, 'I was wondering whether someone might have sabotaged Katrina's mascara . . .?'

'What do you mean?'

'Put something corrosive into the tube so that when she went to repair her make-up, she—'

'Charles, I am sorry, but since Katrina's death I've heard so many fatuous conjectures about how she died that I really don't want to hear any more.'

'Maybe not, but . . .' Charles Paris got the feeling this inter-rogation wasn't getting anywhere.

'God,' Geraldine Romelle said suddenly, 'Ned English is such an arsehole!'

As a means of changing the subject, Charles couldn't deny that it was a very effective one. There was no way he could stop himself from asking, 'Why? What's he done?'

'He's just taken me out for lunch.'

'Doesn't sound very offensive so far.'

'No, I agree. It was a very nice lunch in an excellent restau-rant. And Ned kept trying to ply me with alcohol and I kept telling him that I never drink during the day when I'm performing in the evening.'

What an admirable practice, thought Charles, though an unfamiliar one. The idea didn't really appeal to him. 'So what did Ned do wrong?'

'He just kept going on about how successful he was with women.'

'Ah. Yes, I've had a bit of that from him,' said Charles, remembering their conversation at the Ivy.

'Apparently, he's got this incredibly young girlfriend.'

'He mentioned that to me too.'

'And when he told me this, I don't know what he wanted me to do. Slap him on the back? Tell him what a dog he was? What a rogue? What a sex-god? Though I must say, of all the men to whom I might apply that particular description, Ned English wouldn't even make it to the back of the queue.'

'So, apart from crowing about his conquest of the younger woman . . .?'

'Well, I guess he was asking my advice. The thing is, this girl he's with was one of the unsuccessful contestants on *StarHunt*.'

'Really? That I didn't know.'

'Yes, when it came to the final voting, Katrina Selsey got the gig and Ned's girl – called, unbelievably, Billie-Louise – came, I don't know, third or fourth.'

It made sense to Charles, the idea of Ned English using his importance on *StarHunt* as a seduction technique.

'But the impression I got,' Geraldine continued, 'was that, so far as Ned was concerned, the girl was beginning to get rather demanding.'

'Rather in the way that Katrina Selsey did?'

'Yes. From his description of Billie-Louise, she could have been a Katrina Selsey clone.'

'Well, surely he can just dump her?'

'Ah, but this is the problem. Ned reckons he's in love.'

'Oh dear.'

'It's the real thing. All his former relationships have only been groundwork, tedious preparation for the *grand amour* that is Billie-Louise.'

'Huh. God, aren't men stupid?'

'Oh yes,' Geraldine Romelle agreed with something like fervour.

'So what kind of thing is Billie-Louise pressurizing Ned to do?'

'It's entirely predictable. Katrina Selsey won the part of Ophelia in *StarHunt*, Billie-Louise was one of the runners-up. Katrina's no longer on the scene. Ned's the director of the show. Billie-Louise reckons he's in a position to give the part of Ophelia to her.'

'Ah. I see. So Milly Henryson would be out the window?'

'Right. And Billie-Louise apparently argues that the viewing public know her from having gone through so many rounds of *StarHunt* and it'd be great publicity if she took over the role.'

'Which, knowing how besotted people in this country are with anything "from off the telly", might be true.'

'It might, Charles. Anyway, this is Ned English's dilemma. Obviously, for the recasting of Billie-Louise to happen, Tony Copeland would have to agree. And Ned said he took me out to lunch because he wanted my advice on whether to put the suggestion to Tony Copeland or not.'

'Are you particularly close to Tony?'

'Absolutely not! I've been in other productions for his company, yes, but I don't know him more than to say hello to.'

Charles Paris's mind was racing. Suddenly, there was a new candidate for the attack on Katrina Selsey. Ned English was under intense pressure from his teenage lover to get her the part of Ophelia. But that part would only become available when Katrina Selsey was out of the equation. Blinded by household bleach, perhaps. It was certainly an intriguing avenue for investigation.

But he didn't share his new suspicions with Geraldine. Instead, he continued their conversation. 'It is odd then, isn't it, that Ned should have thought you knew Tony Copeland better than he did, that it was worth taking you out to lunch because you might be able to second-guess his reaction to the idea of casting Billie-Louise.'

'Odd, I agree.'

There was a wryness in her tone which made Charles ask, 'Are you implying that there was another reason why Ned took you out for lunch?'

'Oh yes. Being on *StarHunt* has really gone to his head – I cannot believe the size of that man's ego. Having spent the entire lunch maundering on about Billie-Louise and how she's the love of his life, when we're leaving the restaurant he actually has the nerve to come on to me! Wouldn't I like to go back to his hotel for a quick drink, he's always fancied me and . . . What is it with men?'

'I don't know,' said Charles Paris. But, sadly, he did.

'That's what I like about you, Charles,' said Geraldine Romelle, turning her wonderful gold-flecked eyes on him.

'What?'

'The fact that we just get on, we can talk about things, just chat, confident that there's no sexual interest on either side.'

Charles wondered. Had she said that in genuine innocence? Or was it a calculated ploy to deflect any amorous advances he might be contemplating? Either way, it was very effective, leaving him in absolutely no doubt that he was never going to get anywhere with Geraldine Romelle.

'Rod's coming down to see the show on Saturday,' she said, in what, depending on what she had meant by her previous remark, might or might not have been a *non sequitur*.

'Rod?'

'My husband.'

'Ah.' No point in saying, *I didn't know you were married*. 'Is he in the business?'

'Good heavens no. I'm not daft.'

'What does he do?'

'Civil Engineer.' Charles could really think of no comment to make on that. 'We're going to Bristol on Sunday. Our daughter's at the university. Rod and I will ensure that at least one impoverished student gets a large Sunday lunch.'

It was odd; it had never occurred to Charles that Geraldine Romelle might be married. She didn't wear a wedding ring, but that could mean anything in the theatre. And he realized that whenever he met an actress (*actor – dammit!*), he assumed she was potentially available.

Possibly reading his thoughts, Geraldine went on, 'No, I'm lucky to possess that rarity in the theatre – a happy marriage. How about you, Charles? Do you have one?'

'A happy marriage?'

'Yes.'

'Well . . .' said Charles Paris.

NINETEEN

I t was on the train from Swindon on the Friday morning that he thought of ringing Frances. The fact of going up to London planted the idea in his mind. Well, that, and the question Geraldine Romelle had asked him about his marital status.

Frances's mobile was in answer mode, and Charles reminded himself that of course she'd be working. Headmistresses can't take casual personal calls on Friday mornings.

So he was quite surprised when his wife rang back within ten minutes. Her voice sounded taut. 'Charles, are you all right?'

'Yes.'

'Nothing's happened to you?'

'What might have happened to me?'

'Where shall I start? You might have fallen out of a pub and been run over. You might have got sick drinking wood alcohol. You might finally have been diagnosed with cirrhosis of the liver.'

Charles found all this rather offensive. It was one of those mornings when he'd woken up determined to curb his drinking. He firmly intended just to have a couple of glasses with Tibor and Portie at lunchtime, then nothing till a single virtuous pint at the end of the evening's show.

'Thank you. What a charming image you paint of your husband.'

'You're the one who provided me with the brushes and paint.'

'*Touché.*'

'And then, of course, you might have had a backstage accident. Your production of *Hamlet* seems to be getting more and more like *Macbeth*. It's got a curse on it, consistent bad luck.'

'Well, you'll be happy to hear that nothing else untoward has happened since Katrina Selsey.'

'Good. So, to what do I owe the honour of this phone call? And, Charles, if you have the nerve to say you just wanted to hear my voice, I will ring off immediately. You're keeping me from my break-time coffee as it is.'

'Yes. Sorry. I just, um, well . . . I'm on a train up to London and that made me think of you.'

'Really?' Her voice was dry with cynicism. 'And why are you going up to London? Work?'

'Sort of kind of.'

'What does that mean?'

'I'm meeting up with Tibor Pincus.'

'Oh.' Frances was impressed. She knew the Hungarian's achievements in television. 'Well, I suppose that might lead to something.'

'Don't hold your breath. We're meeting up with an actor nicknamed Portie, who was in that telly play I did with Tibor way back. Do you remember him?'

'Portie? Don't think so. What's his real name?'

'Do you know, I can't for the life of me remember. But he's one of the biggest piss artists in the business.'

'Is he?' said Frances coldly. 'Takes one to know one.'

'Now that's not fair.'

'No?'

Charles was silent.

'Where are you meeting them?'

'Joe Allen.'

'Ah. Well, don't drink too much, Charles. Remember you've got to get back to Marlborough and give a performance tonight.'

'It's all right, Mummy,' he said in a little boy voice. 'I'll be good.'

'Huh.' Then his wife changed the subject. 'Is Milly doing all right?'

Of course. Frances in Mother Hen mode, worrying about her former pupil. Charles wished he'd been at a school with a head teacher as caring as his wife. And he remembered wistfully the times when he'd been in a marriage with someone that caring. Before he screwed everything up.

'Milly's fine. Good little actress.' With Frances he didn't need to make the political correction.

'Yes . . .'

There was something in her voice that made Charles ask, 'Why? Have you heard she's got problems?'

'Kind of.'

'What, is this on this Facebook thing? Or Twitter?'

'No, Charles, that's public. Everyone could read that. No, Milly texts me occasionally, and I had one from her a couple of days ago which sounded pretty miserable.'

'Oh yes, that'd probably be Wednesday. I had a chat with her then. She was very low.'

'Why?'

'The boyfriend Sam was having a major telly interview in London. I think it kind of brought home to her that her career was unlikely ever to keep pace with his.'

'Yes . . .'

Again, knowing Frances so well, Charles picked up the nuance in the monosyllable. 'Do you think there's something else worrying her?'

'I did rather get that message, mm.'

'What was it?'

'Well, she wasn't specific, but I got the impression Milly was feeling guilty about something.'

Charles Paris didn't frequent Joe Allen as often as some actors. He rarely worked in the West End which meant he didn't have the geographical convenience – or the money – to use the place as a canteen. But he always felt reassuringly at home when he did go there. There was something engagingly New York about the brick-walled basement, the framed posters of stage shows long ago celebrated and mostly forgotten, and the defiant chirpiness of the waiters and waitresses with white aprons tight around their waists.

Inevitably, Portie was dominating the conversation, particularly after the second bottle of wine. He was one of those actors who was always full on, who appeared to have no introspective setting. Having been frequently described as 'larger than life' he seemed determined to live up to his billing. Charles wondered whether Portie too had those moments of misery and self-doubt when he was alone at three a.m. But

from the way he bigged up his sex life, it seemed unlikely
that he ever was alone at three a.m.

A few years older than Charles, blessed with extraordinarily
good looks and boundless raw talent, Portie had had a charmed
start to his career. Cast in a major television series before he'd
even finished at RADA, he'd gone on to deliver an acclaimed
Prince Hal and even more acclaimed Hamlet at the RSC. When
he moved from the subsidized to the commercial sector, the
success had continued. He had been one of those actors who
make other actors sick. Whatever parts had come up on stage
or television, every director wanted Portie to play them. As
was customary in the theatre, no one considered that it might
be fairer to spread the work a bit more evenly around the
acting community. For many months Portie had been flavour
of the month and nobody could get enough of that flavour.

He relished the celebrity lifestyle too. Once he'd moved
back to London from the relative obscurity of the RSC at
Stratford, his outrageous behaviour quickly made him a darling
of the gossip columns. A wife, one of his contemporaries at
RADA, had been quickly shed, and he had worked his way
through a series of high-profile liaisons. Portie produced the
mandatory illegitimate children, bar room brawls and drunken
appearances at televised awards ceremonies. The tabloids,
starved of characters in the mould of Richard Burton, Peter
O'Toole and Richard Harris by a new generation of actors
who were pretentiously 'dedicated to their craft', couldn't have
been happier. They gleefully took up the nickname 'Portie',
and a day when they couldn't report some new Portie outrage
was a wasted day.

Remarkably, through all this, his talent remained undimmed.
He still was a brilliant actor. Then he was cast as the lead in
a big-budget television drama series opposite that year's flavour
of the month actress (with whom he had the inevitable high-
profile affair). The show took every award on offer and was a
huge international success. It was particularly big in America,
where its stars were fêted and cosseted on publicity tours. Their
high profile led to many offers of work, particularly for Portie.

It was at this point, lured by the prospect of big dollar
cheques and needing to escape rather complicated domestic

circumstances in England, that Portie decided to up his roots and move to try his luck in the States.

What happened to him thereafter was not well documented, at least not in his home country. Reports of Portie's outrageous behaviour in Los Angeles soon dwindled away to nothing. The tabloids found new 'bad boy celebrities' to puff up (and subsequently destroy). Portie was seen in supporting roles in a couple of mediocre movies, but clearly didn't crack Hollywood in a major way.

For all Charles Paris knew, he may have had a perfectly successful career in the States, starring in miniseries and Movies of the Week, but none of his work made much impact in the UK.

Looking at him in Joe Allen, Charles could see that Portie hadn't aged well. The excesses of his lifestyle had taken their toll. Now in his sixties, the famous thatch of golden hair had subsided into a horseshoe of grey above his ears. The distinctive angular face had spread sideways, its skin reddened by broken veins. And the magnificently trim body, which had encouraged so many schoolgirls to pin up photographs of Portie in their bedrooms, was slack with fat. Prince Hal had given way to Falstaff.

One thing, it was clear from that lunch at Joe Allen, hadn't changed. Portie still drank.

And, so long as nobody else wanted to take much part in the conversation, he remained a very entertaining companion. Even if he hadn't made it big there himself, he commanded an inexhaustible supply of scurrilous anecdotes about the biggest Hollywood stars.

Charles Paris was quite content in the role of listener. Though, like most actors, he could take centre stage in a social situation, he didn't crave that kind of attention. In rehearsal he sat quietly at the side of the room with *The Times* crossword. Joining in in moments of communal hilarity, but generally just listening. He eschewed big occasions. The thought of attending a Cup Final or The Last Night of the Proms was anathema to him. In a crowd he became invisible, lost the fragile hold he had on his personality. Outside work, the less people he was with the better. His ideal was one other person, preferably female. Having a meal with a woman he fancied, that was Charles Paris's idea of heaven.

But he could still enjoy being in the company of a born entertainer. And Portie was certainly that. He had just finished a hilarious defamatory story about Dustin Hoffman's monomania when for a moment he waxed philosophical. 'But why shouldn't we draw attention to ourselves during our brief spell on earth? Human beings are by their nature ephemeral, and surely actors are the most ephemeral of all. What do we leave behind? Performances on stage that are forgotten within weeks. Performances on film and television that will soon look dated and whose technologies will soon be superseded. Lovers' memories of ourselves that die when they die. Children? The product of a few randomly scattered but tenacious sperm. Children who grow away from us and forget us.' He refilled his glass and raised it. 'Enjoy the moment – it's the only bloody thing we can be sure of.'

Tibor and Charles raised their glasses too, to toast the thought.

'Still, enough about me,' roared Portie, laughing, knowing it was a joke, knowing that there was never going to be enough about him. 'What about you, Charles? You still getting work?'

'Occasionally. You actually catch me in one of those rare moments when I've got a job.'

'Good for you!'

'I'm doing—'

But he knew the interest in his career would be short-lived. 'Why is it,' Portie cut through his words, 'that all directors are full of shit?'

'Thank you,' said Tibor Pincus, not really offended.

'I don't mean you, Tibor. You were bloody good. You recognized actors' talent and let them display that talent. Let me rephrase my question. Why is it that all directors *nowadays* are full of shit? They all think they know your job better than you do. Some of them have the nerve to give you bloody acting lessons. Particularly in the States, particularly in television. Yes, all right, television's a technical medium, but it's not rocket science. All the director has to do is point the bloody camera at that actor and *let the actor bloody act!*' He looked across at Charles. 'Who's directing the show you're doing?'

'Bloke called Ned English.'

'Oh, bloody hell! I remember him. One of those poncey poseurs who thought, because he'd been to Cambridge and studied Shakespeare, he knew more about the theatre than people who'd learned how to act by bloody acting. Is he still staging plays in fatuous settings? What are you doing? *As You Like It* set in a bloody launderette?'

'No, actually I—'

'I don't know, how is it some of these wankers survive in the business? Ned English – you could tell from day one he was full of shit. It's scandalous that he's still making a living. He should have been recognized long ago for the pile of crap that he is.'

'Did you ever work with him, Portie?'

'Did I? Bloody tried to. When he was the hottest thing in the West End, he cast me in "The Scottish Play".' Portie looked around anxiously, then realized he wasn't in a theatre and said, 'Bloody *Macbeth*. I'd just done my Hamlet at the RSC, Macbeth was a part I'd always wanted to play, so I signed up. But I didn't sign up to play Macbeth in a bloody Chinese restaurant! Kurosawa got away with relocating the play to medieval Japan, but Ned English's attempt to make it about the dynastic ambitions of Chinese waiters just didn't cut the mustard. Thank God it was a short run and out of town. Hardly anyone saw it. Where's he setting the thing you're doing?'

'Inside Hamlet's skull.'

'Oh. Hamlet . . .?' For a moment Portie seemed taken aback, as if he was about to ask something, but he moved on. 'Bloody typical! No, I'm afraid Ned English and me was not a marriage made in heaven.' He waved at a passing waiter. 'Another bottle of the Cab Sauv, please. No, I hated the bastard. All smooth and smarmy on the outside, but he was up to some pretty devious stuff.'

'Oh?' said Charles Paris.

'Had an eye for the girls. Well, nothing wrong with that. All been guilty of that in our time.' Portie roared a roguish laugh, implying a thousand seductions. 'At least I bloody hope we have. But Ned English had a rather nasty way with the old casting couch.'

'How do you mean?' asked Charles. Tibor Pincus seemed long since to have given up participation in the conversation, content just to drink and listen.

'Ned was screwing some young actress in the *Macbeth* company who was playing a Court Lady – well, for "Court Lady" read "Posh Customer in Chinese Restaurant". Damn pretty girl, can't remember her name, lovely tits though. I'd had a couple of nights with her in the first week of rehearsal and I think she was all upset when I moved on, and Ned picked her up on the rebound. Anyway, she was an ambitious little minx and she got to thinking, "I'm screwing the director of this play, surely I ought to be able to take advantage of that?"'

'In what way?'

'The most old-fashioned way of all, Charles. Little tart wanted a bigger part and starts putting pressure on our Ned. No way she's going to get Lady Macbeth, but she reckons she could easily be bumped up to Lady Macduff – you know, have all her "*pretty chickens killed in one fell swoop*". I mean, of course, what I'm talking about was just company gossip but, knowing Ned English, I wouldn't have put it past him.'

'Put what past him?'

'Bide your time, Charles. You should know better than to interrupt a legendary anecdotist in the middle of telling of one of his anecdotes.'

'I feel appropriately reprimanded, Portie.'

'Bloody hope so too. Anyway, what happens is, interval of the Dress Rehearsal poor cow who's playing Lady Macduff falls down the stairs from her dressing room. After that, what else can happen? Ned's bit of stuff, who he's moved up to understudy, has to go on, doesn't she? All right, could have been an accident, but good old backstage gossip says that maybe Ned English helped the original Lady Macduff on her way, to ensure his continuing access inside the girlfriend's knickers. Huh.

'Anyway, dear boys, must tell you about a rather interesting evening I once spent with Nicole Kidman . . . Well, I say *evening*, but it might be more accurate were I to describe it as a *night*, and let me tell you . . .'

But Charles Paris's mind was too full to concentrate on more tales from Hollywood.

TWENTY

A t Paddington it somehow seemed natural to buy a half-bottle of Bell's for the journey back. And, bizarrely, there didn't seem to be any of it left by the time the train drew into Swindon. Charles didn't have much recollection of the cab ride from there to Marlborough.

Possibly as a result of this – though Charles Paris thought it was more because his brain was too full – that evening's performances of the Ghost of Hamlet's Father and the First Gravedigger were not the best they had ever been. So much so that Ned English, who happened to be watching out front for the show, left a message saying he wanted to have a word with Charles afterwards.

Which was actually very convenient.

A pint in the pub nearest to the theatre did make Charles feel more together as he listened to the reprimand from his director. No point in arguing or defending himself. His behaviour had been unprofessional and out of order.

Apparently – though Charles hadn't been aware of the lapse – he'd even mangled Shakespeare's words. Rather than the Ghost saying, '*O wicked wit and gifts*,' as demanded by the text, he had said, '*O wicked git and wifts*,' which, though it hadn't got a laugh from the audience, had very nearly made Sam Newton-Reid's Hamlet corpse.

His apology was appropriately contrite, not to say abject. But, having got that out of the way, Charles Paris was not going to miss his opportunity to interrogate Ned English about Katrina Selsey's death.

'You still with that *StarHunt* contestant?' he asked with apparent casualness. 'Billie-Louise?'

Ned's eyes, behind the circular tortoiseshell glasses, looked puzzled for a moment. Then, reckoning he must have let slip the girl's name to Charles in an unguarded moment, he replied, 'Yes.'

'You lucky dog.'

'She is rather beautiful, you're right.'

'The older man being rejuvenated by the blood of young virgins?'

'Billie-Louise is hardly a virgin.'

'No, but you know what I mean.'

'Yes.' But something in Ned's tone suggested that being with Billie-Louise was not an unmixed blessing. 'You should try it one day, Charles.'

'The younger woman? Believe me, I have. Fine, I've found, till you get on to their taste in music and movies.' He paused, uncertain for a moment how much finesse to use in his investigating, before deciding to plunge straight in. Not feeling very original, he fell back on the approach he'd used with Bazza in The Pessimist's Arms. 'You know how backstage gossip spreads, don't you, Ned?'

He snorted. 'Tell me about it.'

'Well, I heard something about you and Billie-Louise . . .'

'Who from?'

Charles shook his head. 'Never reveal your sources. The rumour was that Billie-Louise was putting pressure on you to get her into the show as Ophelia.'

Maybe it was the booze uninhibiting him sufficiently to be that blunt. His words certainly had an effect on Ned. For a moment the director just mouthed at him, without any sound coming out. Finally, he got himself together sufficiently to say, 'Did you hear that from Geraldine?'

'I said I wouldn't reveal my sources.'

'I bet it was her. She's a devious cow.'

Charles hadn't really thought of her in that light before but, remembering the deftness with which she had neutralized any sexual advances from him, he thought Ned might be right.

'Anyway, so what? What if I am considering putting Billie-Louise in as Ophelia?'

'Well, Milly Henryson for one is going to be extremely upset.'

'Charles, one thing that working with Tony Copeland over

the years has taught me is that you can't be sentimental in this business. If Billie-Louise, because of her *StarHunt* fame, is going to put more bums on seats than Milly Henryson, then for Tony the question as to who should play the part would be a no-brainer.'

'And have you suggested the idea to him yet?'

Ned English looked shifty. 'Not as such, no.'

'Another thing,' Charles continued on the wave of his alcohol-driven confidence, 'that's being said backstage is that Billie-Louise might have had it in for Katrina Selsey.'

'Why?'

'You talked about no-brainers, Ned. Surely that's the ultimate one? Billie-Louise goes through the whole process of *StarHunt*, week by week training, being tested, reckoning all the time she's the best candidate to play Ophelia. She gets to the end of the process, and thanks to the audience vote, the part is given to Katrina Selsey. If that's not a recipe for jealousy and resentment, I'd like to know what is.'

Interestingly, Ned English made no attempt to defend his girlfriend's character from this attack. Instead he said, 'If that were true, in which direction would backstage gossip then lead?'

'Well, since you've been with Billie-Louise at least since the time *StarHunt* ended, people are wondering how long she's been putting pressure on you about playing Ophelia.'

'Meaning?'

'Meaning that having Katrina out of the way would have been very convenient for her.'

This really hit the director hard. 'Are you suggesting that Billie-Louise arranged Katrina's little accident?'

'I am not suggesting anything, Ned. I am merely reporting backstage gossip.' Charles pressed home his advantage. 'And backstage gossip is not suggesting that Billie-Louise arranged Katrina's accident. It's saying that Billie-Louise persuaded you to arrange it.'

Ned English shuddered from this new body blow. 'Have you been talking to Billie-Louise?' he asked.

Charles Paris had never met Billie-Louise, but he didn't think it was the moment to admit that. Instead he replied, 'Maybe.'

'She didn't ask you to do it for her, did she?'

'Do what?'

'Arrange something that would . . . make Katrina unable to continue with the show?'

Stepping further down the track to mendacity, Charles risked another: 'Maybe.'

'Oh God, she's . . .' Ned struggled to come up with the appropriate words. 'Ambitious, I suppose. That's at the bottom of it, but she's so desperate to be part of celebrity culture that she . . . I don't know. I sometimes wonder if there's anything she wouldn't do to get a foot on the next rung of the ladder of fame.'

'But, apart from that, your relationship works all right?'

'It's heaven, Charles.' Through the round glasses the brown eyes looked straight at him, full of undeniable sincerity. Clearly not the moment to mention Ned having come on to Geraldine Romelle after their lunch. 'I love her. I've never felt like this about a woman. I'd do anything for her.'

'Anything?'

'Anything short of doing what she asked me to do to Katrina.'

'She didn't ask you to kill her, did she?'

'God, no. It was just to do something – something that'd stop her being in the show.'

'Did Billie-Louise make any suggestions as to what that might be?'

'No, she left it to me. I think she saw it as some kind of test.'

'Of?'

'Of how much I loved her.'

'Ah.'

'But I didn't do it, Charles! I promise you I didn't. I told her, I'd do anything for her, but not that.'

'And did you respond like that because of your conscience, your high moral standards . . . or because you were worried what would happen if Tony Copeland found out what you'd done?'

Ned English's uneasy shifting in his seat answered Charles's question.

'Do you actually know, Ned, how Katrina Selsey died?'

'Banged her head on the floor.'

'But what made her bang her head on the floor?'

He shrugged. 'No idea, Charles.'

'Well, I don't know this for sure . . . maybe the police do, but they're not about to share their findings . . . but I think someone had doctored Katrina's mascara.'

'Oh?'

'Put bleach or something else corrosive into the tube. When she applied the brush to her eyes, the shock made her jerk backwards. She stumbled over the chair . . . with results that we know all too much about.'

Ned English was thoughtful. 'Sounds like a woman's crime.'

'Mm?'

'Done by someone who knows how women's minds work, how often they tidy up their make-up and so on.'

'Maybe. What would you say to the theory, Ned, that Billie-Louise, realizing there was no way you were going to do it for her, sabotaged Katrina's mascara herself?'

'Doesn't work.'

'Why not?'

'Because the night Katrina died – and indeed the nights either side – Billie-Louise was staying in my flat in London.'

'She couldn't have come down here without you knowing?'

Ned shook his head. 'I spoke to her a good few times every day on the landline.'

'Ah.'

'But,' the director went on, 'if you're right about that business with bleach or acid in the mascara, then I saw something rather interesting that evening.'

'Oh?'

'I didn't think about it at the time, because why should I? But during the first act, after your scene on the battlements – you know, Hamlet and the Ghost, just before the Polonius and Reynaldo scene – I came backstage to give Sam a note. I'd thought of something he could do differently in the Play Scene. Anyway, as I was going into the wings, I met someone who was holding a tube of mascara.'

'Really?'

'Yes.' Ned nodded thoughtfully as a new block of logic

slotted in. 'And it was someone who would benefit very directly from Katrina being out of the show.'

Charles Paris felt pretty sure he knew the answer, but still asked, 'Who?'

'Milly Henryson,' said the director.

TWENTY-ONE

When he woke on the Saturday morning, for some reason Charles Paris didn't have the hangover that his antics of the previous day so richly deserved. Dryish mouth and the shadow of a headache, but that was all. And copious draughts of water dealt with those symptoms.

His condition made him feel perversely virtuous. And his mind was working beautifully.

It would be the *Hamlet* company's last day in Marlborough. A matinee and an evening performance, then the whole bandwagon would move on to Malvern. The skull set would hopefully be re-erected in the theatre there in time for a Dress Rehearsal on the Monday evening, and the play would open to an Elgar-loving audience on the Tuesday. Just one week in Malvern, then on for weeks in Wilmslow and Newcastle before – hopefully – after another week of rehearsal in London, the Tony Copeland production of *Hamlet* would take up its rightful berth in the West End's Richardson Theatre.

In the old days, thought Charles Paris nostalgically, we'd have worked through the weekend and opened in Malvern on the Monday. But astronomical rates of overtime and revised Equity regulations had made working on Sunday a rare event for most contemporary actors. So immediately after that Saturday evening's performance, many of the *Hamlet* company would shake the dust of Marlborough off their heels and be in cars on their way back to London. And those who didn't go then would be off first thing on the Sunday morning.

Charles Paris would be one of the latter group, travelling by taxi and train. He hadn't owned a car since the early, 'conventional' period of his marriage to Frances, when they'd spent much of their time ferrying their daughter Juliet to school, ballet classes, parties and all those other essential social commitments of a young girl's life. It felt like a very long time ago, before the encroachments of working away from home, infidelities and booze had put too much strain on the relationship for Charles and Frances to continue cohabiting. He'd asked himself the where-did-it-all-go-wrong question too many times to bother asking it again that Saturday morning.

Given the natural break in the *Hamlet* production schedule, Charles really hoped that he could unravel the mystery of Katrina Selsey's death before the company left Marlborough. There would be a neatness about that, for one thing. Also, Charles Paris had read enough crime fiction to know how difficult it is to investigate a crime when you're away from the place where it happened.

His optimism about a successful outcome was higher than it had been at any time since Katrina died. Milly Henryson had always been in the frame. Nobody had a stronger motive for getting Katrina Selsey out of the way, and the understudy was already reaping the benefit of her crime by playing the part of Ophelia.

And now Charles had what amounted to a witness statement from Ned English. The director had seen Milly Henryson holding a tube of mascara on the night that Katrina's tube of mascara had been fatally doctored. You didn't have to be Sherlock Holmes to join the dots on that one.

Charles Paris found that crime investigation was very like doing *The Times* crossword. Some days its logic was impenetrable, he couldn't find any verbal links anywhere. Then came the occasional day when he got the first answer the moment he looked at the clue and put in the rest of the solutions almost as quickly as he could write them down.

That Saturday morning felt like one of those *Times* crossword moments. And, as if to confirm the feeling that everything was going his way, the moment Charles had this thought his mobile bleeped, telling him he'd got a text message.

It was from the stage management, listing the day's calls for the *Hamlet* company. The actors were called for the customary 'half', thirty-five minutes before the start of the matinee. But the backstage crew were called for twelve o'clock to plan the get-out after the evening show.

And, of course, as she'd told him in The Pessimist's

Arms, Milly Henryson was still expected to fulfil her ASM duties.

Charles kind of knew that Milly was one of those people who'd be early for things. Well brought up, polite, thoughtful girl. Well educated too – she'd been to a school with a very good headmistress.

So, because he was experiencing one of those rare days when nothing could go wrong, he was unsurprised to find the girl alone in the Green Room when he arrived at the Grand Theatre at eleven thirty. And – another measure of how good a day he was having – she was alone, reading a copy of *The Stage*.

He did not hesitate about going to sit next to her. 'So,' he said, 'soon it'll be goodbye to Marlborough.'

'Yes.'

'And will you leave with pleasant memories?'

She grimaced. 'Some. It's kind of my first professional job in a proper theatre, which is good. And then it's been great, getting my big break, getting a chance to act with Sam. But . . .' Her expression suggested those pluses were outweighed by the minuses.

'Hm.' Charles realized he didn't have time to be delicate in his approach. Soon other members of the stage management team would be arriving. The window for private conversation would be a short one. 'I wanted to talk to you about getting your big break.'

'Oh?'

'It's an ill wind and all that. You get your big break, but what did Katrina Selsey get?'

Milly Henryson coloured. 'Look, obviously I'd rather the circumstances had been different, but I don't have to tell you, Charles, how important a part luck plays in the theatre. Yes, my good luck was a result of Katrina's incredibly bad luck, but it'd be stupid for me to feel any guilt about that.'

'Would it?' asked Charles Paris pointedly.

'What do you mean?'

No time for equivocation. Hit her with the facts. 'During the first half of the show, Milly, the night Katrina died, you were seen backstage with a tube of mascara.'

'Yes.' The girl turned the full beam of her dark-blue eyes on him. She looked completely innocent, but Charles Paris had encountered too much duplicity in his life to be fooled by that.

He was, however, a little taken aback when Milly said, 'I have it with me every night.'

'What for?'

'Well, for Sam, obviously.'

'For Sam?'

'Charles, you know Sam has very pale eyelashes. For them to register onstage he has to use a lot of mascara.'

'Oh?' said Charles Paris, feeling his card-house of conjecture beginning to topple.

'And always when he comes off after his scene with you on the battlements . . . well, it's so powerful, the way the two of you play it . . .'

'Thank you,' said Charles Paris, unable to curb the actor's instinctive hunger for a compliment.

'And Sam almost always ends up with tears pouring down his cheeks, so I stand in the wings with the mascara, so that I can repair the damage before his next scene.'

'Oh. And what do you do with the mascara once you've done that?'

'Put it in Sam's dressing room.'

'So the night Katrina died, what—?'

Charles looked up to see Bazza enter the Green Room. The stagehand scowled at him. The *tête-à-tête* with Milly Henryson was at an end.

Thank God, thought Charles, that I didn't actually accuse her of doctoring Katrina's mascara, that I didn't accuse her of murder.

But that was lower in the pecking order of his thoughts than the main one. With a sickening crunch of logic, Charles Paris realized that every idea he'd had about the case up until that moment had been based on a false premise.

TWENTY-TWO

C harles left the theatre to buy a sandwich for his lunch, then went up to his dressing room to eat it. There was no one else there and there wouldn't be till round one fifty-five, the 'half' before the two-thirty matinee.

His mind was too full to notice what was in the sandwich. He thought back again to the evening of Katrina Selsey's death. Nobody but Peri Maitland knew of the plan to hijack Sam Newton-Reid's dressing room. Milly Henryson had returned the tube of mascara there once she'd repaired his make-up after the battlements scene with the Ghost of Hamlet's Father. There was a perfectly reasonable chance that whoever introduced the corrosive into the tube had effected the sabotage then, before Katrina's invasion. The *StarHunt* winner had never been the target, Sam Newton-Reid had. And, as with Katrina, the aim had been to cause an injury rather than death.

So Charles was no longer looking for someone with a grudge against Katrina Selsey. Now it was someone with a grudge against Sam Newton-Reid.

He rang through to Peri Maitland.

'Charles,' she said before he had a chance to identify himself. Which must have meant she'd saved his number. 'I thought we'd agreed that any conversation between us was now closed.'

'I know we did, but there's something I need to check with you.'

'What?' Her tone was not welcoming.

'Listen, it's going back to the night Katrina died.'

'Surprise, surprise.'

'I want to know about the mascara.'

'We went through all this at the hotel.'

'Yes, but there's something else I need to check. The mascara tube that Katrina used . . . was it definitely hers?'

'I assume so, yes. Why should she be using anyone else's?'

'But, I mean, did she actually take it out of her own make-up bag?'

'No, she picked it up off the table in front of the mirror.'

'And do you recall bringing that from her previous dressing room?'

'Charles, for God's sake! I can't remember every bloody detail. It's not as if I was making a video of what we were doing.'

'No, but—'

'Look, we were in a rush. I was just going along with Katrina's mad idea to avoid another tantrum from her. And we were worried about people seeing what we were doing, so we just grabbed everything from Katrina's dressing room and dumped it in Sam's. Then we grabbed his clothes and bag and stuff and dumped them in Katrina's old dressing room. The whole exercise probably took less than a minute.'

'And did you take anything of Sam's from the table in front of the mirror?'

'I don't think there was anything of his there.'

'But there could have been?'

'What are you on about, Charles? What do you actually want to find out?'

'I want to find out if it's possible that the mascara Katrina used was already on the table when you came into the dressing room.'

'Ah.' Peri Maitland mulled that over for a moment. 'Well, yes, I can see that's a reasonable question to ask. And the answer is: I just don't know. I suppose it could have been. But then again, that wouldn't make any sense. Sam Newton-Reid is a chap, Charles. Dong!' she said in a way he'd noticed young people using to point up a statement of the bleeding obvious. 'Chaps don't use mascara. Or at least some do, but I wouldn't have thought Sam was the type. He seems all red-blooded male, happy with that Milly he's got.'

Charles didn't waste time explaining about Sam Newton-Reid's pale eyelashes. He just said, 'But it would in theory be possible that Katrina picked up a tube of mascara that was already in the dressing room when you entered it?'

'It would,' Peri Maitland replied in a tone of great

exasperation, 'in theory be possible. Though I can't for the life of me see how that could be important. Now, Charles, will you get off the phone and out of my bloody life!'

Charles Paris felt pretty sure now that he had the solution to the mystery. And his view had shifted a bit. He was moving away from the theory that someone had had a grudge against Sam Newton-Reid. Now he was thinking of someone who had a grudge against the whole show, someone whose aim was to mess things up for Tony Copeland Productions. As Frances had pointed out, you can't do *'Hamlet* without the Prince'. And a severe eye injury to the actor playing the eponymous hero could really screw things up.

There weren't many candidates for the role of saboteur. Charles remembered the lines he had heard in The Pessimist's Arms after Jared Root's accident. 'I could also arrange some other accident to screw up your plans.' And then: 'If I don't get more money, you just wait and see what happens.'

Charles reckoned Bazza hadn't got more money, so he'd taken affairs into his own hands.

TWENTY-THREE

Charles Paris came offstage after the matinee battlements encounter with Hamlet to the sight that Milly Henryson had promised him. She was waiting in the wings, soon to enter for her first scene with Polonius. As Sam Newton-Reid came offstage, she had a handkerchief ready to mop up his tears and a tube of mascara to repair the damage to his wood-shaving eyelashes. They stood close as she titivated his make-up, a rather touchingly domestic scene.

Charles went slowly up to his dressing room, knowing that it would be empty and knowing that he needed time to think. He sat heavily in front of the mirror. Framed by the Ghost's helmet, the false-bearded face that stared back at him looked distressingly old.

Bazza. He was now convinced of Bazza's guilt. He remembered the last encounter they'd had in The Pessimist's Arms. Though the details had been subsequently eclipsed by Doug Haye's attack on him, Charles had been surprised at the time by Bazza's overreaction to the accusation of causing Jared Root's 'accident'. But he recalled suggesting that the two events might be linked. If the stagehand had thought he was about to be accused of causing Katrina's death as well, then his response was perhaps not so disproportionate.

The more Charles thought about it, the better Bazza fitted the profile. He might also have had access, amongst all the backstage paraphernalia, to some corrosive substance more powerful than household bleach. Yes, it was definitely Bazza.

Charles Paris's day was still going well, and he felt excited rather than apprehensive about the forthcoming confrontation. He knew the form. He'd acted out such scenes in any number of dire stage thrillers. ('As the Detective Inspector, Charles Paris was about as menacing as a kitten.' – *Coventry Evening Telegraph*.) The gap between the matinee and the evening performance would probably be his best chance to get Bazza on his own.

His mobile rang. It was on the table where he'd left it when he went on stage. The Ghost of Hamlet's Father's armour hadn't been designed with a suitable pocket for a phone.

'Hello?'

'Charles, it's Tibor.'

'Oh, good to hear you. Most enjoyable lunch yesterday.'

'Well, yes, enjoyable for people who like listening to Portie.'

'Oh, he's not so bad. The self-appointed life and soul of any party. Very entertaining.'

'I agree. But like most entertainments Portie's conversation should be of finite duration.'

'Ah, you went on a bit after the lunch, did you?'

'And how. You see, Portie's just landed on me. He asked to stay at my place and I couldn't really say no. He's drinking me out of house and home. Got to bed at four this morning.'

'Ah. With Portie talking all the time?'

'Yes,' Tibor Pincus replied through clenched teeth. 'I didn't get in many words edgeways.'

Charles tried to keep a giggle out of his voice as he said, 'You have my sympathy.'

'And what's more, he hasn't got any money. God knows what went wrong in the States, but he's completely skint. Keeps touching me for the odd twenty.'

'So how on earth did he afford the fare to cross the Pond?'

'His son paid for that.'

'Really? So why's he over here? Just to meet up with his far-flung family?'

'If he's going to do that, with the number of bastards he claims to have spawned, it could take quite a long time. But no, I think he's just come over to see the one son. Which is why I wanted to warn you, Charles.'

'Warn me of what?'

'That Portie is about to descend on you.'

'On me? Why?'

'Because he knows you've got digs in Marlborough and he's reckoning to crash out there.'

'But why on earth is Portie coming to Marlborough?'

'To see his son.'

'His son's in Marlborough?'

'Yes. He's in your production of *Hamlet*.'

'Really?' But even as he spoke, Charles remembered some-thing. Bewilderment gave way to understanding. Portie's real name came back to him. Jeremy Portlock. Will Portlock must be his son.

'Portie's on the train from London as we speak,' said Tibor Pincus. 'He's going to see his son Will in tonight's performance of *Hamlet* at the Grand Theatre.'

'Well, good luck to him. He'll have a long wait. The Second Gravedigger doesn't come on till Act Five.'

'But Will Portlock is not playing the Second Gravedigger.'

'Sorry to contradict you, Tibor, but he is.'

'Not according to Portie. According to him, in tonight's performance, Will Portlock will be playing Hamlet.'

'Oh, my God!' said Charles Paris.

TWENTY-FOUR

Though encumbered by the armour of the Ghost of Hamlet's Father, Charles Paris sped up the stairs to the star dressing room. He now understood everything with remarkable clarity. He was caught up in that oldest of theatrical plots – the understudy putting the actor he's understudying out of commission and thus gaining his moment of glory on the stage.

After Jared Root's accident, Will Portlock had reckoned the part of Hamlet must be his. How much it must have hurt to have Sam Newton-Reid suddenly parachuted into the production. And, given the level of diplomatic skills displayed by Tony Copeland and Ned English, it was entirely possible that no one had even apologized to the understudy for his exclusion from the role.

Will had made one attempt to sabotage Sam by doctoring his mascara. That had gone horribly wrong, resulting in the death of Katrina Selsey. But he wasn't going to risk another failure. He had actually paid to fly his father over from Baltimore to see him play Hamlet that evening. Whatever he'd lined up for Sam Newton-Reid must be something he knew would work.

Charles pulled open the door of the star dressing room and burst through. As he did so, he glimpsed something tall and heavy falling towards him.

Whatever it was struck him on the head.

Charles Paris fell, unconscious, on to the dressing room floor where Katrina Selsey had died.

TWENTY-FIVE

He didn't know how long he was out, perhaps only a matter of seconds. Certainly, there was no one else in the room when he came round.

Gingerly, he pulled himself up on to the chair in front of the mirror. His head was still buzzing; he didn't feel quite there.

Charles looked down to the stone floor to see what had hit him. It was a black-painted metal stand, robust enough to carry the weight of the heavy old-fashioned stage lights. The kind of kit that might easily be found lying around the scene-dock of a place like the Grand Theatre.

The stand had presumably been propped against the wall. A string ran from it to where it had been fixed to the dressing-room door. Charles's opening the door had pulled it down on him. A very effective booby trap.

Thank God for the heavily padded helmet of the Ghost of Hamlet's Father. That had taken the full force of the falling metal and protected him from more serious injury. What the stand's effect might have been on the bare, blond head of Sam Newton-Reid when he returned at the interval Charles shuddered to contemplate. It would certainly have put him out of commission for the second half of the matinee. Would his understudy have been put in to play that second half, or would the rest of the performance be abandoned? Might Will Portlock's triumph have had to wait till the evening performance?

Charles suddenly became aware of the low mumbling from the tannoy which relayed the onstage action to the dressing room. He heard Polonius saying, '*Tell him his pranks have been too broad to bear with.*'

Oh God! It was the start of the Closet Scene. In which the Ghost of Hamlet's Father had to make an appearance. Maybe Charles had been unconscious for longer than he thought. He still felt a bit woozy.

Before he left the star dressing room, he climbed shakily

on one of the chairs and removed the string that had been pinned to the top of the door. He untied the other end from the light-stand, which he propped safely in a corner where it was in no danger of falling on anyone.

Then he hurried down to the stage to haunt Hamlet.

The Ghost gets offstage before the end of the Closet Scene. The action ends with the exit of Hamlet, dragging off the body of Polonius, and that, in Ned English's production, was the cue for the interval to start.

Charles Paris went straight up from the stage to the star dressing room and sat down, waiting for Sam Newton-Reid to appear. When he did, the boy looked puzzled to see the older actor there.

'What's this? Not a repeat of Katrina Selsey's annexation of my dressing room, is it?'

'No, Sam. But it is to do with her death.'

'Oh?'

'Look, if I try to explain, it'll sound completely daft, but would you just trust me on this?'

'OK . . .' Sam responded cautiously.

'Would you mind just not using this room during the interval?'

The boy thought about this, then nodded and said, 'All right. I'll go to Milly's dressing room. I do quite often, anyway. Just get my mascara, that's all I need.' He stepped forward to pick up the tube from the table, just as Katrina had done the night she died. Then he moved to the door. 'I'm not quite sure why you're being so mysterious. You will explain this to me at some point, Charles?'

'Promise.'

'OK.' And a slightly puzzled-looking Sam Newton-Reid left his dressing room.

Charles Paris sat and waited. He felt pretty sure the dressing room would be visited before the end of the interval, and he was right. The door was pulled open very gingerly and, as anticipated, he found himself facing Will Portlock, dressed in his Second Gravedigger tights and smock.

The scene that greeted the young actor was so far from his expectations that for a moment he was dumbstruck. Then he demanded, 'What the hell are you doing here, Charles?'

'Recovering from having a very heavy light stand falling on me.'

'Ah.'

'I know what happened, Will.'

'Do you?'

'Both times.'

'Both? If you think I had anything to do with the accident to Jared Root, then—'

'No, I don't think you had anything to do with that. I'm talking about Katrina Selsey – here in this dressing room.'

'That had nothing to do with me.'

'No?'

'I didn't come in here that evening after Katrina staged her takeover.'

'I'm not suggesting you did. But you came in before she took it over. You came in to plant the tube of mascara there. The tube that you had doctored with bleach. Or maybe to doctor with bleach the one that was already in here.'

Will Portlock hadn't been expecting that. Once more he gaped dumbly as Charles continued, 'You had no means of knowing that Katrina was going to come in here. The mascara was meant for Sam. You didn't want to kill him, just injure him enough so that he couldn't go on playing Hamlet. But your first attempt didn't work.' Charles pointed to the light stand in the corner. 'So you tried again – with something that would cause an even more serious injury. But for a second time your booby-trap caught the wrong victim.'

'Yes,' Will Portlock agreed distractedly.

'I know why you did it, incidentally, Will.'

'Really? Well, it doesn't take much brainpower to work that out, does it? I did it because I wanted to play Hamlet.'

'Yes, but I know why that mattered to you so much.'

'Oh?'

'I had lunch yesterday with your father. With the famous Portie.'

That was a major shock to the young man, for which all previous ones had been mild and ineffective preparation.

'Jeremy Portlock. I've known him so long as "Portie" that I'd forgotten his full name. Will, I know most of the details of what you did. I know that you paid for your father's flight over from Baltimore so that he could witness you playing Hamlet. Which is why you had to get Sam out of the way.'

'I'd play the part much better than he does,' snapped the boy, suddenly young and petulant.

'That may or may not be the case, but it doesn't justify the kind of violence you were planning.'

'What do you know about it, Charles?'

'All I know is that violence very rarely achieves its ends.'

'Oh, really? What you don't know is what it's been like all these years growing up with my mother. With her going on about Portie all the time. Not that he stayed with her long. He'd upped and left before my first birthday. Fairly soon after that he moved to the States. And you'd have thought that would have made my mother hate him. But no, in her case absence certainly did make the heart grow fonder. She still thought "Portie" was wonderful.' He put the name in ironic quotes.

'And for over twenty years I've had to hear just how wonderful he was every bloody day of my life. With the implication, of course, that I was rather less wonderful, that I'd never match up to my father's achievements. So now do you see why I've got to prove myself to him, why I've got to play Hamlet this evening?'

'I can see why you think that, yes, Will, but you've got to face the facts. It's not going to happen.'

'What, you mean you're going to shop me?'

'I don't think I'll need to do that . . . so long as you give me a solemn promise that you'll give up further attempts to injure Sam.'

'But he's got to be injured. Otherwise, how am I going to play Hamlet tonight?' There was an obsessive note in his voice now, and Charles was made aware of just how long Will Portlock had been planning the *coup de théâtre* whose sole purpose was, for once in his life, to impress his father.

'Will,' said Charles patiently, 'you are not going to play Hamlet tonight, and the sooner you come to terms with that fact, the better.'

'Oh no?' Suddenly, from underneath his smock, the younger actor produced a gun. Some kind of automatic pistol. God knows where he'd got it from, but it looked distressingly businesslike. And it was pointing straight at the centre of the Ghost of Hamlet's Father's breastplate. Which sadly, being only made of fibreglass, wouldn't offer much protection from a bullet.

'So what are you planning to do with that, Will?' asked Charles, acting a coolness that he did not feel.

'Whatever's necessary. Silence you, for a start.'

The boy's bravado, learned from action films he had watched, sounded mildly ridiculous, but Charles could see from his eyes that he was deadly serious. The way he was behaving was the product of many years of accumulating slights and frustration. Someone in Will Portlock's mental state was profoundly dangerous.

'Just a minute.' Playing the part of someone cool wasn't getting any easier for Charles. 'You shoot me, yes, all right, that would have the effect of silencing me. But it would also have the effect of getting you charged with murder, and there's no way you can play Hamlet when you're in police custody, is there?'

'I could hide your body,' said Will defiantly.

'Oh, like Hamlet does with Polonius? Yes, great. But it would be found.'

'Not until after I've done tonight's performance.'

'And is that all you care about?'

'Yes.'

'Will, you're not being very logical. For one thing, I might not tell anyone what I know about what you've been doing. I might be silent on the subject of my own accord. So silencing me by shooting me would be taking a completely unnecessary risk.'

The pointing gun wavered for a moment while the boy took this on board.

'Then again –' Charles pressed home his advantage – 'shooting me is a diversion. It's not bringing you any nearer to your primary ambition, which is to get Sam Newton-Reid out of the way.'

'I could shoot him too.'

There was still something slightly comical about Will Portlock's confrontational manner, but Charles wasn't laughing. The more the boy talked, the more unhinged he sounded.

'Double murder? Hiding two bodies? I think you'd be found out pretty quickly. And that would be the end of your career as an actor. The end of your career as anything except the inmate of a prison cell. I'm sure you don't want to take that risk.'

'I want to play Hamlet tonight,' Will repeated doggedly, 'so that my father can see that I'm as good an actor as he was.'

And Charles realized just how dissociated the boy was from reality. From the one performance he had done in the role at the Tech, it was evident that, though he might be an adequate actor, Will Portlock was never going to come near the volatile and sparkling genius of the young Portie. Which was probably the root of all his problems.

But the fact remained that Will was still pointing a gun at Charles and, in his manic state, was quite capable of using it. He needed talking down into a more manageable mood.

'Listen, Will, I think you're getting things a bit out of proportion. You must see that you can't—'

The door suddenly opened to admit Sam Newton-Reid. 'Sorry. I've just remembered I need my cloak for the Fortinbras scene.' He moved to take it off the hook, not noticing the gun in Will Portlock's hand. Until he turned round and found it pointing straight at him.

'How very convenient, Sam,' said his understudy. 'I don't have to come looking for you.'

'What are you playing at, Will? Is this some kind of practical joke?'

'No, by no means, Sam. I've never been more serious about anything in my life.'

'Will,' Charles remonstrated, 'this has gone on quite long enough. Stop this charade before you do something stupid. Put the gun away and we'll say no more about—'

'Put it away? Just when I've been offered the opportunity of a lifetime?' Will Portlock smiled at his intended victim.

'I'm sorry about this, Sam. I've got nothing against you personally, but I'm afraid you have to be removed from the
equation.'

'Are you saying you're going to shoot me?' Sam asked in
bewilderment.

''Fraid so.'

Suddenly, Sam Newton-Reid looked really terrified. Charles
had seen him looking scared every night when they first met
on the battlements of Elsinore and he shouted out, '*Angels
and ministers of grace defend us!*' but that was just acting.
This was the real thing.

Aware of the fragility of Will's mental health, Sam asked,
'But why? Why do you want to shoot me?'

'Because,' came the predictable reply, 'I have to play Hamlet
in tonight's performance.'

'Well, fine. I'll step aside. I'll tell Ned I've got some gastric
bug. I'll—'

Will took a moment to assess this proposal, before twisting
his lips wryly and shaking his head. 'Shooting you would be
more secure. Then I can play Hamlet for the rest of the tour.
And in the West End.'

'There's no chance Tony Copeland'll let—'

'Shut up, Charles!' Will Portlock screamed, before turning
back to his proposed victim. 'Sorry, Sam, but this is the way
it's got to be.'

'You can't! You mustn't do it!' Tears were now glinting
through Sam Newton-Reid's mascaraed eyelashes. 'Think of
the effect it'll have on my parents! And on Milly!'

Will Portlock shook his head again with great seriousness.
'Some things are more important than personal feelings. There
are some things that just have to be done.' And he lowered
the gun to target Sam's chest.

Charles Paris didn't know what to do. He felt he should
jump Will, knock the gun out of his hand. But, encumbered
by the Ghost of Hamlet's Father's armour and still dizzy from
the blow to his head, he knew he couldn't move quickly enough
to get away with it.

'Goodbye, Sam,' said Will.

At that moment the dressing room door was pulled open to

reveal a slightly swaying Portie. Instantly, the pistol disappeared back under Will's smock.

Portie ignored his son and Charles Paris. Instead, he addressed Sam Newton-Reid. 'God, you don't look a bit like your bloody mother.'

'What?' asked Sam, still shaken by his recent jeopardy.

'Still, I can see from your costume that you are actually playing Hamlet and you are in the star dressing room. That's a step. I thought you might have made the whole thing up in some pathetic plea for attention.'

'I think you've got it wrong, Portie.'

'What have I got wrong? God, is that you, Charles, under the coal scuttle and the grotesque beard?'

'Yes.'

'I should be on stage,' said Sam Newton-Reid. And clutching his cloak around him, he scuttled out of the dressing room.

'I'm Will,' said the boy. 'I'm your son.'

'Then why the hell is somebody else dressed as Hamlet?'

'It's rather complicated. This is just the matinee. You see, I—'

'Oh, don't bother me with explanations! Anyway, what is that costume you're wearing? Who're you playing in the bloody farrago?'

'The Second Gravedigger,' Will Portlock replied humbly.

'Huh,' said his father. 'Bloody long way I've come to see a Second Gravedigger.'

TWENTY-SIX

There were a lot of empty seats for the matinee of *Hamlet*, and the Gravediggers' scene didn't get as many laughs as it usually did with a fuller house. There's a tipping point in the number of people who have to be present for them to find Shakespeare's groan-worthy puns funny, and that afternoon the Grand Theatre audience hadn't reached it. When they came off stage at the end of the scene, without any discussion of the matter, a very subdued Will Portlock followed Charles Paris to the latter's empty dressing room.

'Have you still got the gun with you?' asked Charles as he sat down wearily.

'No, I put it back in my bag.'

Will sounded listless and defeated. Charles was struck, not for the first time, by how good actors are at hiding their real emotions when they're on stage. A few minutes before Will had been mugging away in his customary Mummerset style as the Second Gravedigger. Now he looked as if he'd been run over by a truck.

'Where did you get it?'

'The gun? Through a friend at drama school. It was a prop one.'

'You mean it didn't work?' Charles asked with some annoyance. 'You mean I've just been in a blue funk about a gun that was a dummy?'

'No. My friend knew something about guns. He converted it back. It works all right.'

Charles felt rather relieved that at least his recent panic had been justified.

'It's no good, is it?' said Will Portlock moodily.

'What's no good?'

'Everything. But mostly me trying to get some kind of relationship going with my father. He doesn't care about me. He never has cared about me.'

'I don't think Portie's ever been great at facing up to his responsibilities,' said Charles tactfully. 'Or caring for people.'

'No. He's a bastard. He's always been a bastard. I should have recognized that a long time ago.'

Charles couldn't think of anything to say. So he just shrugged.

'The basic thing a father should do for his child is actually to *be there* when the kid's growing up.' A pang of guilt ran through Charles as he recalled how remiss he'd been in fulfilling that parental duty to his daughter Juliet. But it wasn't the moment to beat himself up about that. Will Portlock was still talking.

'If I'd accepted early on that I was never going to see him, that he would never be a part of my life, I think I'd be less screwed up than I am now. And with my mother constantly putting him on a pedestal, I always had this pressure to be like him, to see if I could match his talent . . . And I should have accepted long ago that I was never going to do that either. My talent is a very modest one.' Charles didn't contradict him. 'I've learnt that since I've actually been working in the theatre. I've seen lots of people with more talent than me. But I suppose I can go on in the business, never hitting the heights, never getting the big break.'

'Lots of actors do,' said Charles gently.

'Like you, you mean?' Which wasn't actually precisely what Charles Paris had meant. But Will was too preoccupied to realize the rudeness of what he had just said. He sighed and went on, 'I don't know that I've got the energy. I only went into the theatre because of him. To try and emulate his achievements. I should have known I hadn't got a snowball's chance in hell of doing that.'

There was a silence, then Charles asked, 'Did Portie say anything helpful, you know, when I left the two of you in Sam's dressing room to change my costume?'

'Did he hell? The bastard only tried to touch me for some cash. And the minute I'd given him a twenty, he announced that he was going straight back to London.' Poor Tibor Pincus, thought Charles. 'Didn't even wait to see me as Second Gravedigger. Just went on about the "bloody inconvenience" I'd caused him by dragging him down to "bloody Marlborough".'

'Ah. So you have no plans to meet again?'

'Never!' said Will Portlock with great vehemence. 'I'm going to work hard on forgetting that I ever had a father!' Then in a softer tone, he asked, 'The thing is, Charles, what are you going to do about it?'

'How d'you mean?'

'You know what I've done. You know about the bleach in the mascara, the light stand booby trap. I've threatened you with a gun. And I threatened Sam too.'

'Mm.'

'And the awful part of it is . . . that I probably caused Katrina Selsey's death.'

'You didn't intend to.'

'No. So it wouldn't be murder. Murder has to involve intention.'

'You've been reading up on the subject?'

'I have. I've been in such a terrible state since it happened. Feeling the most awful guilt.'

'And yet, in spite of that, a short while ago you were pointing a gun at Sam and saying you were going to kill him.'

'Yes,' Will agreed in a bewildered tone.

'And if you'd done that, there'd have been no question about your intention. And, of course, you threatened me too.'

Will Portlock nodded and then pressed his fingers against his forehead as if trying to rub away some memories. 'I've been in a most peculiar state since I started working on this production.'

'Yes, I think you have.'

'But going back to Katrina, all right, it's not murder, but I think I could possibly be done for manslaughter.'

'I'm certain that you could.'

'So that's why I want to know what you're going to do. Some people in your situation would feel they'd have to go to the police and tell them what they knew.'

'Yes, some people would,' said Charles judiciously. 'And, of course, there's another possibility . . .'

'Oh?'

'That the police's own investigations might find out what really happened to Katrina and how you were involved in it.'

'Yes. Obviously, I've thought of that.'

Charles Paris was silent for a moment. Then he said, 'My instinct is to leave the police to it. Let them do their job. I don't feel particularly inclined to help them. What you were trying to do to Sam was pretty shabby, but I do understand your reasons for doing it. And yes, you probably did cause Katrina Selsey's death, but that was a tragic accident. There is no way you could have foreseen it happening. So, as I say, my instinct is to leave well enough alone. And I'll have a word with Sam. Tell him you've been under a lot of strain. Ask him to keep quiet about what happened this afternoon in his dressing room.'

'Is he likely to agree to that?'

'I think I can persuade him to do so.'

Will Portlock slumped in his chair with relief. He looked totally drained.

'But one thing I would say, Will, is that you're not well. The way you've been behaving suggests that you need help. You've been under a hell of a lot of pressure for a long time. I think one of the conditions for my silence might be that you go and see a doctor, try to get some psychiatric help.'

'It's something I have considered.'

'Then why haven't you done anything about it?'

'My mother . . .' He winced, as if under renewed strain. 'My mother says only weaklings believe in mental illness. She says Portie would never have gone to a doctor if he'd been feeling out of sorts. He'd just get on with things.'

'Yes,' said Charles softly. 'Portie'd just have another drink and get on with things. But what he might do is not your concern. You're not Portie. For the rest of your life, Will, you're not going to care about what Portie might do.'

'You're right.' A weak smile crossed the boy's features. 'I'm not.'

There was an air of tension in the cavernous auditorium of the Theatre Royal, Newcastle. It was the Tuesday, the day of the first public performance of *Hamlet* in the final venue of their tour, and the entire company had been called at two o'clock to be addressed by Tony Copeland. They hadn't seen the producer since Marlborough, though his assistant, Doug Haye, had attended the First Nights in Malvern and Wilmslow. Charles Paris and Doug had not spoken, perhaps both unwilling to remember their encounter in a Marlborough alley.

Charles looked around at his fellow actors. Dennis Demetriades, he noticed, had shaved parallel lines in his sideburns to give a striped effect. In spite of his tigerish facial hair, the young actor looked as anxious as the rest of the company.

Charles himself didn't feel tense that afternoon. His default setting was the anticipation of bad news and, as the tour progressed, he had become less and less optimistic about the chances of this *Hamlet* transferring to the West End. In Malvern and Wilmslow they'd had pretty good houses and some enthusiastic reviews – particularly for Sam Newton-Reid – in the local press. But, having been in a similar situation many times before, Charles didn't feel the momentum that accompanies an inevitable transfer. There had also been ominously little publicity for a show which was supposed to be on its way to the Richardson Theatre. According to the Twitterati in the company, the only story 'trending' about anything to do with their production of *Hamlet* was a constant stream of bulletins from Jared Root saying how quickly he was recovering from his injuries and how good his new album was going to be. (And Charles now knew those messages were probably emanating from Tony Copeland.)

He had talked to Geraldine Romelle about his gloomy prognostications, and she had seemed to share them. But he hadn't expressed doubts to anyone else in the company, not wishing to dampen the youthful enthusiasm of people like Sam and Milly, excited about what they believed would be the next step in their glittering careers.

On the dot of two, Tony Copeland and Doug Haye appeared onstage. There were no chairs there for them. They had travelled up on a morning train and would be going straight back to London after Tony had made his announcement. As ever, he looked more accountant than impresario.

The actors' chatting dwindled to silence at his appearance and he went straight into his statement.

'Ladies and gentlemen, thank you for coming and I hope you have a good performance tonight. Thanks for all the hard work you have put into this production and congratulations on a very successful tour. After the early disruptions in Marlborough, this *Hamlet* has turned into a very good show.

'As you all know, there was a possibility of the production transferring to the Richardson Theatre in London. The factors governing my decision about the transfer are mainly financial. I don't need to spell out to you the costs of opening any show in the West End, and Tony Copeland Productions are not in the business of losing money.

'The planning of this production from the start has depended on publicity generated by the *StarHunt* television programme and the casting of Jared Root from *Top Pop*. With neither him nor Katrina Selsey in the cast, we've lost that publicity boost. This, may I say, is no reflection on the talents of the actors who have taken on their roles, both of whom have done an excellent job, which has been recognized by some very positive notices on the tour.

'However –' Charles knew there was going to be a 'however' – 'the financial prospects for this production do not justify the expense of taking the show into the West End.' There, he'd said it. 'So the West End options in your contracts will not be taken up, and the production will close at the end of this week here in Newcastle.

'I realize some of you will be very disappointed by this news, but you can't argue with hard financial facts. I'd like to thank you all once again for your talent and hard work and wish you good luck with wherever your careers take you next.'

With that Tony Copeland and Doug Haye left to catch their train back to London.

On his return from Newcastle Charles Paris reverted to the half-life of an unemployed actor in Hereford Road. He didn't keep in touch with anyone from the *Hamlet* company. An actor's social life is like that. During a production you see the same people every day for months. You eat with them, drink with them and (if you get lucky, which Charles hadn't this time) sleep with them. Then, the minute the production ends, that tight social group instantly unravels. There's nothing callous or unpleasant about this parting of the ways; it's just the way it is.

If you were to meet one of the company by chance somewhere, you'd have a drink and reminisce about what fun it had all been. But, unless you'd contrived to get involved emotionally or just sexually, you wouldn't make any effort to arrange further meetings. Then you'd meet some of them on other productions, where new intense exclusive social groupings would form.

Through theatre friends and acquaintances Charles did hear news of some members of the *Hamlet* company. And through a major publicity campaign of newspaper and television ads, not to mention huge posters on the sides of buses, he heard about the show that Tony Copeland Productions took into the Richardson Theatre. As the producer had threatened in Marlborough, he brought in a programme of music featuring the winners of the recent series of *Top Pop*. Headlining was the previous year's winner, Jared Root, who had made a remarkably quick recovery from his onstage injuries and whose 'accident' was milked shamelessly for publicity. The coincidence of the production's First Night with the release of Jared's new album was a PR man's dream.

The show was full every night with television viewers, many of whom had never been inside a theatre before. Thus yet another West End venue failed to find space for a straight play.

And nobody would ever know at what point during the production of *Hamlet* Tony Copeland had made the decision that the show wouldn't transfer to the Richardson Theatre. Or if that had been his plan right from the start.

Charles Paris never reported back to Tony on the conclusions he had reached about the death of Katrina Selsey. To do so seemed pointless, somehow. And Charles felt increasingly convinced that the responsibility he had supposedly been given was an aspect of yet another of Tony Copeland's power games.

Another television series of *StarHunt* was set up, this time eschewing the dangerous area of stage plays and going for the safer option of finding a new star to play the lead in a revival of a popular musical. Needless to say, Ned English wasn't

required as a judge for that. His brief period of television
celebrity was over and, Charles heard from a mutual acquaintance, Billie-Louise very quickly dumped him in favour of a
producer who could do more for her career.

One day, a few months after *Hamlet* closed in Newcastle,
Charles Paris opened his *Times* to see a photograph of Tibor
Pincus looking out at him from the obituary page. The text
was lavish in its praise for the director's groundbreaking work
in the early days of television drama. There were fulsome
tributes to his talent and skill on radio and television, many
of them from the very broadcasting executives who had failed
to give him any work for the final two decades of his life, or
even to answer his calls.

A friend passed on to Charles the details of the arrangements for Tibor's funeral. He intended to go, but somehow
didn't get around to it.

A few months later Charles Paris was mooching around
Hereford Road, trying to engage with a particularly intransigent
Times crossword, when he had a call on his mobile.

'Hello?'

'Hi, Charles. This is Will Portlock.'

'Oh. Good to hear you. To what do I owe this pleasure?'

'Well, partly . . . all right, I'll come straight out with it. I
just wanted to check that you hadn't changed your mind.'

'About what?'

'About what we talked about in your dressing room in
Marlborough . . . that time . . .'

'About shopping you to the police?'

'Yes.'

Charles chuckled. 'That's not the kind of thing I'd change
my mind about.'

'I'm glad to hear it. Sorry, I should have trusted you, but
you know how worries and mad ideas go round in your
head.'

'Yes,' said Charles, remembering some of the mad ideas
that had gone round in Will Portlock's head. 'And you haven't
heard anything from the police, either in Marlborough or
anywhere else?'

'No.'

'Then I reckon, Will, that you've got away with it.'

'Bloody hope so.'

'Anyway, what're you doing? Got any work?'

'Not theatre work, no. I've given it up.'

Charles thought that was probably good news. 'Oh?' he said.

'I never really liked it that much. Nor was I very good at it. I only went into the theatre because . . . well, you know the reasons.'

'Yes. So what are you doing?'

'I'm starting an accountancy course next month.'

'Really? What does your mother think about that?'

'I don't give a shit what my mother thinks. I don't see her now. She really is a profoundly silly woman.'

'Oh. Well, you sound a lot better than you did in Marlborough.'

'I took your advice, Charles. Went to my doctor. He reckoned I was very near a breakdown and put me on some medication which seemed to work. And now I'm having some cognitive behavioural therapy – it's really getting me sorted out.'

'That's good to hear.'

'How about you, Charles?'

'What?'

'Any work?'

The 'No' was instinctive. But also accurate. 'Heard anything from anyone else in the *Hamlet* company, Will?'

'Not much. Oh, I ran into Sam in the West End last week.'

'How's he doing?'

'Back in telesales.'

'Oh dear.'

'But his big news was – Milly's pregnant.'

'Really?'

After Will ended the call Charles tried not to feel depressed by the news about Sam. But the young man's likely future was far too clear to him. Telesales had been meant as a short-term fix, but with a baby on the way, the demands of bourgeois responsibility could all too easily lock him into that or some similar job with a regular salary. And so another great acting talent would remain unfulfilled. The enduring unfairness of the theatrical life asserted itself once again.

Not that that surprised Charles Paris under his carapace of cynicism in Hereford Road.

'So there never was a murder?'

'No, Frances, there wasn't.'

They were sitting in a Hampstead Italian restaurant. In happier times it had been one of their regular haunts. In happier times they had often drunk too much there and stumbled back to the family house, then fallen giggling into bed together with carnal intentions. But that evening, with Frances looking at her most headmistressy, those happier times seemed a long while ago.

'Freak accident,' Charles went on. 'The girl tripped over the chair backwards, didn't have a chance to cushion her fall, fell straight down on the stone floor.'

'Hm.' Frances nodded and toyed with her tagliatelle. It seemed inconceivable after all these years, but there was an awkwardness between them, as if neither could think of what to say next, as if they were *making* conversation. Maybe there were just too many subjects which, over the years, had moved off limits.

'Juliet OK?' asked Charles.

'In very good form.'

'And the twins?'

'Getting bigger every time I see them.'

'Mm.' He didn't ask after the welfare of his daughter's extremely boring husband Miles. Instead he took a substantial swallow of their favourite Sangiovese. 'I'd like to see them.'

'Nothing stopping you,' said Frances drily. 'You have a phone. You have their number.'

'Yes.' Another topic he should perhaps not have ventured on. The pang which Will Portlock's talk of a father's responsibilities had brought to him returned more forcefully.

Probably mentioning the 'C' word would be equally fool-hardy, but he took the risk. 'Will you be going to Juliet's at Christmas?'

'Possibly,' replied Frances.

'Only possibly? I thought that was a kind of regular annual fixture.'

'I may be going to the States for Christmas.'

'Oh?' God, now Charles really wished he hadn't mentioned the subject. Distantly, he remembered a time when Frances had had some male friend in California. He had never been told the level of intensity of that friendship, and he'd never asked for more information. Which had been sheer cowardice on his part. Charles Paris would always rather remain in ignorance of things that might hurt him.

Except, of course, that very ignorance actually hurt him. Why couldn't he just come out with the direct question? Ask Frances if she was seeing someone else? Ask the identity of the person who she had a 'lunch date' with when he'd phoned her that Sunday from Marlborough? But he shirked the responsibility of all such enquiries.

Maybe that was the only thing in life Charles Paris had ever been good at. Shirking responsibilities.

'Anyway, Frances . . .' He topped her up with the Sangiovese. It was a mere gesture of politeness – her glass was nearly full – but a little ritual he had to perform before refilling his own empty glass. 'We must do this more often.'

He knew, even as they came out of his mouth, that they were the wrong words. Once again, Frances responded with a cold, 'Why?'

'Well, just because we . . . because there has been so much between us.'

'Has been,' she echoed, without much intonation.

'Mm.' A silence, unlike other silences that had come between them over the years. 'Oh, by the way, Frances . . . Did you hear that Milly Henryson's pregnant?'

'Yes, she texted me.'

'Ah. Right. Of course.'

Their conversation for the rest of the meal was on general topics. Neither wanted coffee. They both even refused the complimentary glasses of sambuca which had been so much a ritual of previous visits to the restaurant.

Frances had her car outside – perhaps part of the reason why she hadn't drunk much. They kissed chastely on the lips before she got in. Charles promised to be better about keeping in touch and said he'd ring Juliet.

As he watched his wife drive away, Charles Paris felt more desolate than he had at any time in his life.

He made his way to the tube. Back to Hereford Road. Back to the inadequate consolation of a bottle of Bell's.

In time, they aired the series about the Civil War presented by the feminist academic with big breasts. Charles watched the episodes with great attention until he got to the one about the Battle of Naseby. Though he recognized small details of the costumes he had worn at Newlands Corner, the footage had been shot in such tight close-up that no one could have identified the actor or actors involved in the historical reconstruction. Had Charles Paris been the kind of actor organized enough to produce a show reel of his greatest performances, there would have been no point in including that one. He felt a sensation of guilty relief that he hadn't urged any of his friends to tune in to watch his 'latest telly'.

And so the months rolled on. The phone didn't ring from Maurice Skellern's office. Or from anywhere else much. Charles Paris, continuing to worry about such matters as an appropriate male response to the large breasts of feminists, drank too much Bell's whisky. And kept meaning to phone Frances. And his daughter Juliet. But somehow didn't.